FUTURE PERFECT
(TENSE IN SPACE)

Vol.16 of Indian Creek Anthology Series

Future Perfect (Tense in Space)
Volume 16 of the Indian Creek Anthology Series

Published by Southern Indiana Writers, 2200 Reno Ave., New Albany, IN, 47150
Book designed by T. Lee Harris

ISSN 1085-357X
ISBN 978-0-578-06278-5

Cover design by T. Lee Harris

Cover Photo by NASA, ESA, and the Hubble SM4 ERO Team

CONTENTS

5   By the Light of the Silvery Moons........................... T. Lee Harris
            Illustration.. T. Lee Harris

21 Real Image .... Marian Allen

22 Effective Camouflage .... Ardis Moonlight
            Illustration.. T. Lee Harris

25 Designer Genes .... Dirk Griffin

26 Space Oddity .... Ginny Fleming
            Illustration.. T. Lee Harris

39 Alien Universe .... Jeannine Baumgartle

40 Solo For Multiple Instruments .... Marian Allen
            Illustration.. Marian Allen

53 Metamorphic Space .... Ardis Moonlight

55 Soul Speak .... Glenda Mills
            Illustration.. T. Lee Harris

61 Over Time .... Jeannine Baumgartle

62 Red .... Joy Kirchgessner
            Illustration.. T. Lee Harris

69 Infinity, Eternity .... Marian Allen

70 Quantum Toast .... Ginny Fleming
      Illustration.. T. Lee Harris

77 Lonely is the Night .... Dirk Griffin

78 Universe Time .... Bonnie Abraham
      Illustration.. T. Lee Harris

89 Greensleeves .... Jeannine Baumgartle

90 Rebel .... Samantha Lopez
      Illustration.. T. Lee Harris

102 Mixed Metaphor .... Marian Allen

104 Vibes .... Jeannine Baumgartle
      Illustration.. T. Lee Harris

112 Infinity Dances .... Dirk Griffin

113 Mergers in Space .... Carl Page
      Illustration.. T. Lee Harris

132 Contributors

BY THE LIGHT OF THE SILVERY MOONS

T. Lee Harris

The twin full moons' eerie silver light sucked color out of everything, making the familiar streets of New Chicago look strange to Sergeant Lloyll Apogee. She didn't like strange. Not many cops did.

Moonlight also bathed the well-appointed courtyard of one of the city's high-end residence blocks. As she watched, the last of the gawkers wandered back inside, the open doorway spilled golden light against the silver, stretching the retreating three-legged shadows long over the imported grass and manicured landscaping. The door closed, abruptly cutting off light, music and the babble of voices leaving only the light of the moons. It lent the area a deceptively peaceful, pastoral look — that is, if you ignored the uprooted shrubbery, smashed flower planters and churned up soil that marred the perfection of one corner of the yard.

She closed her eyes, clenched her fists and took a deep breath, sucking in the familiar scents of the police cruiser: her Canid partner's grooming powder, coffee, spicy fast food and faux leather. Counting slowly to ten, she released the breath, opened her eyes and called up the cruiser's on-board computer system. A small, holographic keyboard appeared in front of her. Placing her fingers over the virtual keys, she managed to type a few words before her fists clenched again. She hated writing reports. She hated it almost as much as she hated domestic calls. Domestic calls that involved a triad of Kyjolians cranked up the scale a bit. Domestic calls involving Kyjolians during their three-week Solstice Festival shot the meter off the scale.

She grabbed her coffee cup and took a pull on it. The ceram-mug had done a pretty good job keeping it warm, but the rich liquid did little to calm her down. Most of the year, working this upscale

5

sector was a dream, but the last week and a half had been insane. This domestic dispute they'd just dealt with had been all too typical. When she and her partner, Sergeant Euff Gral, arrived, the three spouses were in the courtyard in front of their home bugling inarticulately and throwing things at each other. Large things. Kyjolians' tri-lateral anatomy and heavy world origins gave them immense strength. They usually concealed it well, combining a sharp intelligence with a pleasant demeanor that made them the perfect merchants throughout the Alliance. However, when Festival arrived, all bets were off. No givil beans were in evidence during her inspection of the premises, but she was betting booking's tox screen would be farther off the meter than her piss-off factor.

Privately, she wanted to round up every damned Kyjolian a week before Solstice and shove them all in cryo pods. If they kept them in stasis through Festival, police overtime would be halved at least. She was torn about what to do after the celebration passed. She waffled between turning them loose until the next Festival and shooting them into space, cryo pods and all, to orbit whatever Alliance world they came from until the system's star novaed. Currently, she leaned toward launching them. She'd never voice that opinion or she'd wind up spending yet another month with NCPD's Sensitivity Coach. She rubbed the new bruise ripening along her jaw thoughtfully. The primary spouse of the triad had clipped her a good one as she was trying to clamp the restraints on him—her—it—whateverthehell it was.

Resolutely, she plunked the ceram-mug back into the holder and glared at the keyboard glowing patiently in front of her. Her duty belt creaked against the cruiser's pilot seat as she sat forward to resume her carefully emotionless report.

"How's it going, Lloyll?" Euff asked. As soon as they'd gotten back to the cruiser, Euff had jacked his seat back as flat as it would go and lay with eyes closed, dog-like muzzle pointed at the roof of the vehicle. Claimed it cleared his senses. It was his usual reaction to a bad call—and this one had been spectacularly bad. She'd taken a clout on the jaw, but Euff, being the larger target, had been dodging flying patio items.

"Not bad," she lied, fingers hovering over the keys. "Do Kyjolians have actual eyes? I mean—will it make sense if I say the

Tertiary was repeatedly punching the Secondary in the eye when we arrived on the scene?"

Euff's large, fur-tufted ears twitched in thought. "I dunno. Why not just say the Tertiary was beating the shit out of the Secondary when we arrived? That's what I'd do."

Sergeant Gral didn't fill out reports, claiming his Canid digits were too thick and clumsy to work the keyboard of the onboard system. This was total crap, but Lloyll let it slide. Whenever he'd been forced to write one, it wound up getting kicked back to the senior member of the team for clarification. Senior member. That was her. She viewed writing them herself as cutting out a step.

"Yeah. I know you would." She resumed typing. What the hell? If she got the body part wrong, the Captain would just kick it back for clarification. So much for the skipped step.

She was putting finishing touches on her antiseptic prose when the cruiser's com crackled. The night dispatcher had one of those sexy, breathy voices that was a pleasure to listen to no matter what sex or species you were. "Unit Thirty? Report in, Unit Thirty."

Great. Now HQ was hailing them. She gritted her teeth and kept typing. Euff pretended to be asleep. He was definitely pretending; he snored a helluva lot louder when he really was. It was probably just booking wanting their paperwork. The wagon would have delivered the angry triad to the station a while back. Tough. They could cool their heels in the holding tank a little longer.

The com crackled again and the voice changed from velvet to brass. Captain Sellers, himself, had grabbed the channel. Unlike Apogee's own heavy world mutt lineage, the Captain was pure Terrran human and strictly no nonsense. He sounded even more irritated than usual.

"Apogee! Gral! One of you lazy slugs pick up! Sensors say you've been sitting in the same spot for fifteen minutes."

Lloyll hit Send on the compscreen, watched the little animation of an old-style envelope whiz away, then touched the icon next to the com. The green LED for the live link winked on. "Apogee here, Captain. The incident report should be at booking now."

"Screw the incident report, Sergeant, we have another call close to your current location. We got a body. There's a pair of uniforms helping to secure the area and crime scene techs are already working it, but you two need to haul your sorry asses over there to take charge of the investigation. Now."

Apogee stifled a swearword. "Close to their current location" probably meant more Kyjolians and more givil beans. Glancing at the timepiece in the dashboard, she said, "Sir, our shift is over at the top of the hour—"

Captain Sellers interrupted. "Looks like you'll get a nice chunk of overtime, then. Report back here when you've assessed the situation. If I have to call again, you'll both be pulling Officer Friendly safety duty for the Educational Liaison for the foreseeable future. Got me?"

Apogee grunted. That seemed to be enough, but Sellers raised his voice. "Gral?"

"Yes, Sir!" Even the Sergeant's voice was at attention.

"Then, why aren't you moving, people?"

The address was a little more than a block from the domestic, but it took them blessedly out of the Kyjolian neighborhoods to a cluster of condominiums surrounded by high walls. The rookie cop at the gate was trying to keep the few rubberneckers at a distance. He looked comically relieved as they pulled even and lowered the windows. "Man! Am I glad to see you guys. Head on in, they're waiting for you."

"Hey . . . ," she checked the name plate. ". . . Yoshinoya. Who's already here?"

He waved a hand back through the gate. "CSI bots are all over the place and my partner is in the lobby with some of the residents."

She parked the cruiser beside the Medical Examiner's transport, popped the hatch and frowned at the banks of bright lights that ringed the lawn beyond. Techs rarely expended that sort of wattage without good reason. Her eyes slid to her partner, "Bad?"

Euff's sensitive nose was already wrinkled and his lips pulled back in a grimace. He nodded without a word.

With a sigh, she stepped out, straightened her duty belt and headed toward the lights. Reluctantly, Gral followed. Half-way across, Apogee caught sight of what had wrinkled her partner's nose. The body sprawled on a terrazzo walkway a few meters from the north face of the building. Stopping short, she found herself suddenly wishing for the kinder silver moonlight instead of the brilliant floodlights that threw everything into sharp focus. He—or she—it was hard to tell at that point—must have fallen from a pretty good height given the urk factor. Even without Canid senses, it was bad. Her own misleadingly pert nose wrinkled. "Well, it's called terminal velocity for a reason."

"Actually, Sergeant Apogee, the term doesn't refer to the force at which a falling object hits. It's really a term from fluid dynamics wherein a falling body accelerates—"

"Thanks, Twenty-Seven," she interrupted the slightly mechanical spiel of the CSI drone now hovering down to the opposite side of the remains. "It was a joke and not a very good one."

"Ah. I see. I'm still not very good at recognizing humor, but I'm working on it."

Behind her, she sensed Euff's discomfort. CSI drones sort of creeped him out. Lloyll could see his point. The drones looked like hovering eggs, almost featureless but for the unit's number embossed in the surface. They were imprinted with the persona and intelligence of a real person. Some of the personas really took hold to become what could only be called personality. Twenty-Seven was one of those.

Choosing to focus on the featureless robot rather than the mess at her feet, she said, "Okay, what do we have?"

"Humanoid. From the genetic markers and bits of bluish scale-like skin, a male of the Viboran species. Massive trauma due to blunt force from impacting with the pavement after passing through a plex-ply window." Twenty-Seven shot a red pointer beam at a spot high up on the main building's face. "That one. Twelfth floor. That's our primary crime scene."

Apogee gave a low whistle. "That took a lot of force."

"Agreed. Two of my satellites are already documenting the DB and crime scene inside."

Euff shook off his discomfort. "Wait. There's another body up there?"

"I am afraid so, Sergeant Gral. Double murder. The one upstairs will be a much simpler task than this one. Human. Single projectile shot to the head."

The officers squinted up at the barely visible window. Apogee asked, "How long before we can work the scene—either of them?"

Twenty-Seven gave a thoughtful little hum and seemed to scan the area. "This one will take a while longer due to its . . . scattered nature. The one upstairs, should be—" Another hum, then, "Ah, my satellites have just finished the preliminary scan of the primary crime scene. You can access it now."

Walking into the lobby was like entering another world. The building's designers intended it that way. Color and lighting was warm and muted with antique over-stuffed furniture and potted plants pulled from all corners of the Alliance and beyond. The doors didn't so much shut as whisper closed behind them. It wrapped itself around Apogee like a comfortable cocoon. It made both officers edgy.

A small knot of residents of diverse races perched on the chairs and sofas in one corner of the room. A tall, willowy female Canid officer stood taking notes on a hand-held pad. Apogee recognized her as Sergeant Mauma Aruna. No surprise she'd been paired with the rookie outside. Aruna was one of the best training officers in the NCPD.

Aruna looked up as they entered, spoke a few more words to the fidgety, ancient humanoid male she'd been speaking with and came over to meet them. "Hey! Glad you're here. I'm just about done with statements here." She jerked her head toward the elderly human. "That's the neighbor who called it in."

"He have anything useful for us?" Apogee asked.

Aruna shook her head and deftly paged through her notes using her claw on the hand-held's screen. "Doesn't look like it. Heard loud noises and thought it was another loud party. Apparently, there have been quite a few of those. He was working up to call in when he heard a couple huge crashes. Ran out into the hall to complain and found the door hanging by one hinge. Here, let me shoot this data to your com." A few punches of the claw and Apogee's shoulder com beeped softly.

She pulled the unit down and skimmed. "Hmmm. He didn't see anyone in the hall."

"Nope. You want to talk to him now? Any of them, for that matter. I had them all wait here until you gave the okay to release them."

"Has anyone secured the scene upstairs, yet?" Apogee asked.

Aruna shook her head. "'Fraid not, Lloyll. There were already rubberneckers at the gate when we got here so I planted the rookie in their way. I got mobbed with scared residents as soon as I hit the lobby."

"And Twenty-Seven is processing evidence solo," she sighed. "Typical for a New Chicago night at mid-Festival."

"Ain't that the truth?" Aruna said. "I'm counting the days to Festival's end, then I'm off to a beach somewhere. Been saving vacation days since last year just for this."

"I hear that," Gral murmured.

"Looks like you've got all we'll need for now. Contact info is here if we need to talk to anyone later. If someone needs to leave the building, see if you can escort them around the mess in the courtyard. Twenty-Seven has enough to deal with without adding sight-seers to the mix." She closed the com and replaced it on her shoulder strap. "Efficient job as usual. Thanks, Mau!"

Aruna grinned toothily and looked pointedly at Gral over her shoulder as she exited. "No problem, Lloyll. Some Canids aren't technophobes."

Lloyll slid a mischievous glance at her partner. "Funny how Aruna doesn't have any trouble with keypads."

He sneered. "Her paws are a lot smaller than mine."

"Uuuuh huh. C'mon. Let's get upstairs."

The elevator hissed open onto a hallway blocked by a massive NCPD guard-bot. Stepping onto the plush carpeting of the hallway, they both waited for the bot to scan the ID chips embedded in their badges. After a second, it said, "Identity confirmed: Sergeant Lloyll Apogee. Sergeant Euff Gral." It stepped noiselessly aside like a blue and silver gate swinging open.

It didn't take a leap of deductive logic to locate their destination. Expensive faux-wood doors lined the well-appointed hall with the exception of one that hung by one hinge out from the wall like a torn and bloody fingernail. As they approached, one of Twenty-Seven's satellites hovered out and moved slowly down the hall, apparently scanning for trace evidence. Just outside the apartment, Apogee steeled herself and took a deep breath—which might have been a mistake. The stench of death was stronger here than it was outside.

Ducking under the yellow crime scene banner, they found

themselves amidst total chaos. Furniture and objects lay broken on every visible surface and several colors of blood were spattered and smeared throughout. The second victim lay sprawled in the center of what used to be a luxurious living room with a magnificent view of New Chicago's skyline. Now a stiff breeze blew through the broken window, tossing bits of paper and fabric around and, thankfully, diluting the smell. It looked like a small hurricane had wrecked the room, leaving the raised dining area and kitchenette miraculously untouched.

Finding a section of wall without obvious spatter, Apogee leaned her shoulders against it and waited. She usually let Euff take the lead in investigations like this one. He hadn't been on the force as long as she had, but you just couldn't beat Canid senses for stripping away the layers of a crime scene. It was what made Canids such stellar police officers.

Gral picked his way over to the body and knelt beside it. "This sucker went down before all hell broke loose. All the spatter and breakage is on him, not under him—except for here. Looks like someone went through his pockets."

Apogee pushed away from the wall. "Robbery gone wrong? Kind of extreme for that."

"Hey, Twenty-Seven," Gral said glancing up at a hovering mini-egg. "Have you run ID on this guy, yet?"

In answer, beams of light shot out from the little drone to scan the human's face and an outflung hand. "Accessing Alliance Criminal Identification System. Processing fingerprint and facial scans. Milo Belvy. Age: 52 Sol years. Place of birth: Sol system. Earth. Record for minor offenses, confidence scams and Ponzi schemes in various sectors of the Alliance. Arrested on charges of theft by deception in three systems. Served one year. Early release due to time off for good behavior. One count of petty larceny on—"

"Thanks, Twenty-Seven," Apogee interrupted. "I think we get the drift of what this guy was mixed up in. Send the files to our coms and we'll look them over later. Any other info that might be pertinent?"

"Hmmmm." The silver and white ovoid hovered soundlessly for a few more seconds. "Ah. Closest known associate: Viboran native, Sessem Shikane."

"Viboran?" She chuckled. "Hey, Euff, any bets the mess

downstairs turns out to be Shikane?"

Gral snorted. "Do I look like a sucker?"

Twenty-Seven said, "Do you want the list of Sessem Shikane's offenses? It's remarkably similar to that of Milo Belvy."

"I think we can give it a miss."

"Sending to your coms."

"Thanks."

She turned to make another remark to Gral and was surprised to see him intently sniffing the air. Putting a digit to his lips, he stood, drew his weapon and made for a narrow, darkened passage leading off the dining area. With a sinking feeling, she realized he must've scented someone else in the apartment. Damned rookie mistake to not secure the scene before checking the body. Everyone was stretched to the limit with the non-stop overtime, but mistakes like this could kill you. Without another thought, she followed suit.

Moving softly wasn't easy for a heavy-worlder. Her mass was at least double that of a normal human her size, but with practice, she could do a passable job of it. She caught up with Euff at a door half-way down the corridor. He noiselessly opened it and slipped through. She followed, finding herself in a cluttered utility room.

Threading through stacks of boxes, old electronics and piles of dirty laundry, they crossed to a partially-closed louvered door at the far end. In a lightning move, Euff threw back the door and pointed his weapon behind the environmental control unit. "Come on out. Hands where I can see them."

A muffled whimper answered, "Don't shoot. I didn't do anything."

After a moment of grunting and shuffling, a short, dumpy human with lank dark hair stood and stepped out of the closet. The shaking hands he held over his head were red with blood.

A bright beam of light scanned the man, making him wince. Apogee hadn't even realized the CSI drone had followed with them.

Twenty-Seven said, "Erwin Mustela. Age: 48 Sol years. Place of birth: Sol system. Mars Agricultural Colony 142. Record for electronic misdemeanors, petty theft, breaking and entering. Currently on probation for shooting a public transit bus—"

"A bus?" Gral was incredulous. "You shot a *bus*?"

"Look, it was all an accident," Mustela said. "There was this guy—my girlfriend kicked him—then she . . . it wasn't even my gun, okay?"

The two sergeants stared at him open-mouthed.

"There's a juvenile record, too," Twenty-Seven continued with a tinge of glee. "It's currently closed, but I could request to have it opened."

"No need, Twenty-Seven," said Apogee. "Just send what you have to the coms."

"Done." She could have sworn there was disappointment in the words.

As they escorted Mustela back down the hall, Apogee heard Gral muttering, "Beep, beep, bang, bang" then snickering. He was all business when they reached the dining area, though. Pulling a chair out from the table, he set it facing the living room—and the body, then motioned for Mustela to sit down.

The man looked at the scene, gulped and said, "I need to get out of here."

Gral shook his head. "You're not going anywhere, pal." He pointed to the chair again.

Mustela still resisted. "What do you want me for? I haven't done anything."

Apogee stepped forward and put a hand on Mustela's shoulder. The pressure buckled his knees and he sat down heavily, looking surprised. "So you keep telling us, but you're covered with blood. That looks bad, don't you think?"

"You guys think I killed Milo?" He shot a nervous glance toward the carnage. "Why would I do that? He still owed me for a commerce site I built for him."

"Okay, so how did your hands get bloody?"

"I—I only wanted my money. I came in and found him . . . like that."

"So you rolled the body."

Mustela looked miserable. "He owed me a hundred marks."

Apogee pulled out a chair and sat astride it. "Maybe you better tell us what happened."

"I'm a Coder. A real good one. About a year ago, Milo Belvy

hired me to make some adverts and to build three commerce sites for Arcadia Immersive."

Gral leaned forward. "Isn't that the new Immersion game company? I think I've seen the vid ads for them. Planetary Conquest or something."

"Yeah," Mustela nodded eagerly. "The one with the giant Destroyer-bot blowing the armored troop carrier apart? That was mine."

Apogee frowned. She rarely played games. "Ummm. Yeah. Back to your involvement, this was part of what you wanted to be paid for? The advert?"

"No, it was Sessem who actually hired me to make the ads. He paid me for it up front. The other partners had nothing to do with that."

"There's someone involved other than Shikane and Belvy?" Apogee asked.

"Oh, yeah. Tsuril Izao. I didn't deal with him much—especially lately. He's a Kyjolian. It's Festival so, he's way out of the loop."

Apogee glanced at Gral: "Kyjolian."

Mustela looked at her funny. He said slowly, "Yeah. Kyjolian. You know, the big guys with three of everything."

Gral nodded. "Yah. We know the guys. So what happened tonight?"

"Tonight I was trying to finish the first commerce site when Milo called and told me to stop working. I said okay, but I wanted to be paid for what I'd done."

"It took you a year to complete one site?" Gral said.

"Hey! It was brilliant work. You can't rush genius."

"Right," Apogee said. "So you told Belvy you wanted paid."

"Damn straight. I contracted three hundred for three sites, so I figured they owed me at least a hundred. Milo told me I'd have to take that up with Sessem, that he had all the money."

"So you came here? To talk to Shikane?"

"Yeah—only when I got here, the door was busted and the place was wrecked. Milo was on the floor and there was no sign of Sessem."

Gral's whiskers twitched. "Did you look out the window?"

"Huh?" Mustela looked questioningly at the offficers.

Apogee turned to a new line of questioning. "How much cybernetic augmentation do you have?"

Mustela still stared blankly.

Apogee repeated, "How much augmentation do you have?"

"Cybernetics?" Mustela whined. "Oh PLEASE! I don't have enough money to pay rent, how could I afford body augmentation?"

"Confirmed," Twenty-Seven said. "I can find no cybernetics other than a computer interface."

"Okay, so he doesn't have the strength needed," Apogee sighed.

"Also, blood pattern is transfer, not spatter," Twenty-Seven added.

Apogee nodded, then asked Mustela, "Who else would have a reason to throw Shikane out the window—and the strength to do it?"

The confused look continued for a few beats, then Mustela's eyes tracked to the shattered window and nearly bugged out of his head. "Sessem? Is. . . ."

"Dead," Apogee finished for him. "Very dead. Falling twelve stories onto a pavement has a way of doing that."

Mustela turned white, then took on a greenish tinge. He just kept staring at the broken window.

"Wanna tell us what really happened, now?" Apogee prodded.

Slowly, the man's eyes slid from the gaping window and onto the police sergeant's face. He nodded slowly. "Yeah. I'll tell you everything I know, but you gotta protect me."

They waited, the wind whistling between the broken shards of plex-ply filling the silence.

Finally, Mustela sighed and seemed to fall in on himself. He said wearily, "Like I said, Milo called me earlier tonight to tell me to stop work on the sites. And he did tell me that I needed to talk to Shikane if I wanted to see my money. Then he said that if I wanted to talk to him, I'd better make it fast because Sessem had drained the Arcadia accounts and booked passage on a flight off-planet tonight."

Apogee said, "And?"

"I'd been working with Sessem on another . . . errrr . . . private project. I logged in and found out everything was gone from there, too. I kind of flipped out for a little bit. Then I got over here as fast as I could and—" Mustela broke off abruptly and his face took on an even less healthy color. "Oh man. I must have just missed whoever killed Milo and Sessem. If I'd been a little earlier. . . ."

"A private project." Gral loomed over the Coder. Gral was wiry, but he could loom with the best. He snarled. "Ooookay, I'm tired of getting the story in installments. I think we ought to drag his sorry ass downtown."

"Wait!" Mustela said. "My van. It's downstairs. I have backup copies of all the files and transactions hidden in the back. Everything. Even the . . . other stuff I did for Sessem."

Gral grinned. It wasn't pretty. "Thinking about a little blackmail, were we?"

"I just wanted my money. That's all. Just my money."

The van was at the back of the apartment complex in a littered and smelly alley. It was so beaten up and decrepit, it would have been in danger from the trash pickup units. Even the mitigating effects of the silver moonlight filtering between the buildings couldn't disguise its poor condition. As Mustela unlocked the vehicle and shoved aside a rumpled sleeping roll and empty food cartons, Apogee realized the man was living out of it. She was leaning forward, trying to see into a floor compartment Mustela had just opened when the pavement shook and an all-too familiar bugling split the air.

She whirled to face a Kyjolian blocking the end of the alley, trumpeting angrily and flailing its three powerful arms wildly, sweeping industrial-sized garbage bins aside like they weighed nothing. No doubt this was Izao, the missing Arcadia Interactive partner and much the worse for wear. As if to confirm, Mustela cut loose a piercing shriek and tried to throw himself across the back seat of the van. Gral caught him by the collar of the jacket and hauled him out.

Tsuril Izao grunted with effort and lifted a full dumpster over his head. Another grunt and he flung it. Apogee and Gral dived behind another dumpster, dragging Mustela with them. The heavy steel box crashed into the back of the van, crushing the rear hatch and causing a shower of garbage.

Another angry bugle resolved itself into: "Mustela! You double-crosser!"

"Call for backup," Apogee said, standing and shaking trash off. "I'll keep our friend occupied."

Gral nodded, already speaking rapidly into his shoulder com.

Apogee stepped into the center of the alleyway and held up her badge so it glinted in the moonlight. "Just a moment, Sir. Sergeant Lloyll Apogee of the New Chicago Police Department. I need for you to calm down and tell me what the problem is."

Izao's answer was another bellow. "Betrayer! Where is the money?" Uttering an ear-splitting howl, he lashed out, smashing a few more garbage cans.

The same strength and intelligence that made Kyjolians, as a race, excellent merchants, when used to different ends, also made them some of the most dangerous criminals. Now, with Tsuril Izao wavering unsteadily in front of her, black blood leaking from a hole in his midsection, reeking of gore and givil beans, Lloyll was very sure she was in the presence of the second type.

Stepping closer to the angry Kyjolian, she braced herself for a charge. Her own heavy world ancestry gave her an edge to withstand an onslaught from this tri-lateral wall of flesh, but she'd still have to be careful. Izao outweighed her by a considerable amount and Kyjolians could move fast on those three stumpy legs.

"Mr. Izao, let's talk this over. Do you want to file a complaint against Mr. Mustela? I can do that for you. Just tell me what the problem is."

Use of his name swiveled all three of his sensory stalks in her direction. Even in the moonlight, she could see their angry flush.

"You want to know the problem? Ask him," slurred Izao. A powerful arm thrust at Mustela where he cowered behind Gral. "He knows where the money went. He was in it with Shikane!"

She took another cautious step closer. "Tell me your side, Mr. Izao. Mustela told us part of it and it's hard to ask Shikane. He's dead. Thrown out the window of his apartment. Any idea how that happened?"

Apogee caught movement of two dark shapes down the alley behind Izao. She did her best not to register them as she continued to talk. "Why would Mr. Mustela have any idea where the money was? All he did was design commercials and games."

"Is that what he told you? Didn't he tell you about the special work he did for Shikane?" The sensory stalks wobbled back toward Mustela. "Tell them about THAT, Primate!"

No good. She needed to get his attention off Mustela. She

stepped back into his line of vision—at least she hoped so. With the three sensory stalks waving so wildly, it was hard to tell. "You didn't answer my question, Mr. Izao. What can you tell us about the death of Sessem Shikane?"

The Kyjolian's angry trumpet reverberated off the dingy walls of the alley. The breeze from the near miss of a powerful arm lifted her close-cropped blond hair. She'd been ready for it and had stepped out of reach. Izao bellowed again and charged. She'd been ready for this, too. Dropping to the squalid pavement, she doubled up and threw herself forward, catching his foremost leg just above the knee allowing momentum to carry her all the way through. Izao pitched forward, landing hard against another dumpster that crumpled under his weight. From the shadows, Aruna and Yoshinoya surged forward with a riot stunner and heavy-duty restraints. They never got to use them.

In a surprisingly fluid move, Izao hauled himself upright and heaved the ruined trash bin at them, his outrage blending with the crash of metal against metal as it slammed into Mustela's van completing the destruction the first impact had begun. Aruna and Yoshinoya flattened against the pavement barely missing being crushed by flying debris. The stunner and cuffs skidded away across the pavement.

Apogee was bracing for another charge, when suddenly a white shape dropped from above. "Cover!" Twenty-Seven called.

Instinctively, Apogee ducked as a brilliant light so bright she could see it through closed eyelids flashed for an instant. Izao's scream of pain brought her up to find him doubled up, sensory stalks pulled almost back into his head. Wasting no time, she snatched the restraints from where they had fallen and snapped them closed on the three massive arms. Gasping for breath, she pulled out a small white card. "Tsuril Izao, you have the right to remain silent—"

A muffled voice from behind Sergeant Gral asked, "Hey! Am I gonna get a new van out of this?"

The officers shouted in unison, "NO!"

Captain Sellers flicked pages past on his desk's data screen. "So Mustela wound up spilling the whole story?"

"Oh yeah," Gral said. "We rode Mustela back in the same transport as Izao. By the time we got here, he couldn't talk fast enough to get it all out."

"Belvy recruited him to work on gaming sites, then Shikane recruited him for another job," Apogee added. "They hacked into some of the largest Alliance banks, wormed into some big corporate accounts, artificially inflated the balances, then siphoned off the bogus funds into Shikane's account back on the Viboran homeworld. No one's quite sure what happened after that."

Sellers shook his head. "I see the Forensic Accounting people are all over this already. They're calling it Cyber Counterfeiting. New take on an old game, I suppose." He closed the file with a jab of his forefinger. "Anyway, it's out of our hands now. Before I forget, Sergeant Aruna is going to be fine, but she'll be wearing dark glasses for a while and I'm told Twenty-Seven is still recharging."

"I had no idea the CSI bots could concentrate a strobe like that," Apogee said around a stifled yawn.

"I doubt anyone else did, either. Good job, people. Now, get the hell out of here."

REAL IMAGE

Marian Allen

That photo of the Earth from space is everywhere;
On posters, tee-shirts, magazines—
Not to mention ads
     for everything
          from soap to Save the Whales,
Her global beauty packaged as a come-on.

Gaia, the cover-girl.

Real Image previously appeared in **Byteland Poetry Anthology**
and **PanGaia Magazine**.

EFFECTIVE CAMOUFLAGE

Ardis Moonlight

A couple walked across the parking lot to the sidewalk in front of the chain restaurant. When a glint of light flashed on the man's sunglasses, he glanced up. "Look at that balloon—it's all silver!"

She shielded her face and squinted. "Looks like the kind that people buy for celebrations."

Playfully, the man said, "No, Brenda, that's a UFO. Little green spiders are inside, driving their strange little ship. They're checking out Earth. Effective camouflage, huh? Even has a string hanging, so you'd think it had blown away."

Brenda laughed. "You have such an imagination, Danny! Let's go eat."

Danny kept watching the object, and then winced.

"What's the matter?"

"I don't know." Danny held his fingers over his eyes. Tears streamed down his face.

Brenda frowned. "Are you okay?"

"No. My eyes hurt. God, they hurt."

"Let's go inside the restaurant. Maybe a cold compress will help."

Danny grimaced and followed Brenda. He felt like needles were piercing his eyeballs.

The questionable toy sailed away, undisturbed by the wind pushing in the opposite direction, and drifted low over a small park with swings and a slide.

A three-year-old blond boy with hair to his shoulders stared up and screamed, "Maaamaa, I want the pretty bloon!! Maaamaa!"

A teenage girl and her Irish setter ran past the boy. The dog barked as she leaped into the air, reaching for the string, but it dangled just out of her reach. The dog stopped jumping around; he whimpered and held his tail and head down. The girl's twin sister watched. When the balloon floated over and was just a few inches above, she caught the string, and quickly released it, shouting, "Ow!"

Her twin rushed over with the dog close behind. "What happened, Judy?"

"I swear, Jane, the string shocked me!"

As the dog licked Judy's hand, she felt the pain lessen. That was so weird, she thought. What kind of balloon was that?

The unusual object traveled above the street, nearing webs in trees, webs along roof eaves, and dipped over fields where tunneled webs glistened in the light. The balloon vibrated, its color changing from silver to green and back again, as it encountered each of the spider creations. Then the balloon soared upward, nudging against a tiny spider on a floating silken strand. The spider hissed. Instantly, the camouflaged toy repeated its color vibration change then continued its ascending flight, and settled on a passing jet's wing.

A businessman tapping on his laptop squinted when a glare appeared on the computer screen, glanced out the window, and did a double-take. A balloon all the way up here, he thought, that's really strange. Why wasn't it blowing off the wing? His computer beeped— he glanced at the screen. When he looked back out, the unusual visitor was gone. Had he really seen anything?

The airy object rushed in its descent, then slowed and drifted above a zoological park, then dived close to a building with a sign that read, *Poisonous Animals*. Assuming the shape and color of a small blackbird, the intruder followed a family of six children and two adults as they entered the building. The bird darted around the lobby, zipped through the glass door of the insect entrance, whizzed along the hall, pausing in seconds by each exhibit window, until it reached the one labeled "Atrax—A Funnelweb Spider of Australia—One of the most dangerous spiders in the world."

As two adults entered the dimly lit area, their five-year old boy darted toward the bird. The large glass window shattered at the exhibit. A ten-inch long spider jumped at the boy. He screamed and ran out of the area, followed by his terrified parents. The bird zoomed around the spider, which hissed and jumped at the bird. In a blink of an eye, however, the spider leapt backwards into the exhibit, was reduced to its original size, and the glass returned to the window frame, smooth and flawless.

In a few minutes, a guard and an exhibit staff person, carrying a box, walked cautiously into the narrow hallway. The guard played the flashlight beam along the floor and up to the once-shattered exhibit. He murmured, "I don't see anything. Nothing seems to have happened."

"I'm glad," the woman said. "Sometimes people get really frightened in this building and their imaginations take over!"

While they double-checked the exhibit, the bird fled through the closed doorway and the front entrance. All the visitors were standing nearby watching, but no one noticed the flight through the glass. The moment it flapped over the crowd, someone yelled, "The bird got out." The people applauded as the bird flew rapidly out of sight.

The changeable object rushed higher and higher until the earth became a round, blue ball nestled in the galaxy's black. Enlarging until it was thirty feet in height, the bird changed its color and shape into a muted pink star with five points.

Within the soft, yellow interior, hundreds of spider-like creatures waved four of their eight thin limbs over panels of colors. Their turquoise bodies glowed, happy with their mission. Though they didn't speak, except for small grunts now and then, their thoughts zipped back and forth.

So disappointing. Atrax didn't understand us! She wanted to eat us! The spiders on this planet think about food all the time. Our ancestors were just like that. Perhaps the next planet will have more advanced spiders.

Our mission advisor was accurate about using the bird and balloon shapes. But the advisor was lacking in information. Why was the humankind so interested in a balloon? It was a child's toy. I can understand small humans being fascinated, but the large humans— why did they want to stare at it or catch it? Advisor needs to acquire more data before other missions are made to this planet.

Their thoughts created euphoria, and lit up the red panel that absorbed what they had experienced. With a loud hiss, the starry vessel disappeared into the blackness.

DESIGNER GENES

Dirk Griffin

walking the helix
imagination released
seeking by instinct
a flow of ideas

ascending the ladder
carelessly floating
and recombining
unnaturally

building the unknown
from disparate pieces
a new age coming
from old now reformed

SPACE ODDITY

Ginny Fleming

Have you ever wondered if there's intelligent life elsewhere in the universe? Well, wonder no more. There's life. Intelligence? That's debatable.

I'm David Feagle, and I'd just been ejected from my "mother-ship" at approximately five miles above the surface of some God-forsaken planet about which Uni-NASA had a brain fart. Perhaps "ejected" is a poor choice of words. "Ejected" implies I might have had some say in the matter. Might, if you will, have been allowed access to the controls on my landing module. "Thrown out on my ass" would be more like it.

So there I was... five miles above this purple-blistered planet, trussed up like a Thanksgiving turkey, with my only remaining (or usable) sensory organs being my eyes, and their reports of the swiftly flashing digital readouts told me I was soon to crash land on this hot-pinky-purple blob. Why was I *hog-tied* into my "Space-Lazyboy"? . . . let's just say when you're invited to the Uni-NASA-Big-Dog's 4th of July party, don't get so wasted you mistake an expensive Koi pond for a pretty and decorative urinal. It can get your ass blasted into space—to boldly go where you *never* wanted to go—quicker than snot on a river rock.

Thanks to the high from the Uni-NASA approved intravenous drugs running into my arm, I'd slept most of the journey, and I was still a little fuzzy-brained. So, my mind was consumed with just a touch of panic after I'd come-to enough to note the dash numbers on my sweet ride swirling with growing urgency. Alarms were blaring and my constant companion from lift off (the onboard computer) gleefully trilled the chorus from that old Broadway show: "The circle of *llllife!!!*" it warbled. Geez. Why'd they have to install a swishy computer module?

When it'd finished a two-chorus short-version of the Lion King's theme song, it addressed me as if we were old pals. "Dave, sweetie—be a dear and take note. We're nearing our goal in . . . oh, I dunno . . . couple'a miles? Didn't this flight go fast? Haven't we had just the bestest time *ever?*"

"Mmmuphered!" I answered. . . .oh—did I forget to mention I'd been gagged shortly before lift off? Damn Uni-NASA and their brain farts.

So, as I tumbled the remaining three miles down, safe in my "studio apartment" of a landing module, Swishy the computer filled the month-long minutes singing every word of "We're Off To See The Wizard"—until I wanted to scream, but—if you've been paying attention you'll realize—I couldn't. I closed my eyes and thought of England. Yes, it's true. So true. In space... no one can hear you scream. Or cuss. And frankly, no one gives a damn if you do. Least of all Swishy.

The landing was hard. Made me say: "Rrrrumph" and "Mmmugwhup" and "Wwhaxafrucxal" before the egg-shaped landing capsule righted itself like a Weeble. Within seconds, before I could clear the Tilt-A-Whirl from my head, a gleaming Swiss Army Knife-thingy shot out from the control panel and sliced though the duct tape binding my hands. I immediately rubbed my wrists to get my blood circulating and went for the gag stuffed in my mouth, then I ripped the intravenous drip from my arm.

Swishy trilled his excitement: "Oh, what a *bea-u-tiful* morn-ning! Oh, what a *bea-u-tiful* day! I've got a—"

"Notice to all swishy computers," I snarled an interruption, "There will be a two minute silence in honor of our auspicious landing."

". . .bea-u-tiful *feelll-ing*—everything's go—what's that Dave?"

"I said: Cut the crap, Swishy. No more Broadway until I can get my bearings, capish? Which, if I may translate, means: ' Your alternative is death. Do you understand?' . . .well . . . do you Swishy?"

There was silence for the first time in multiple light years. Finally he . . . her . . . it whispered. Dejectedly. "Whatever you say, Dave. You shoulda said something if it's your time of the month. I'd've understood. I'm programmed that way."

"Did you just now hear me use the word *'death'* in my last communication?"

"Why, yes. Dave, I believe I *did* hear that word. My 'hearing' is quite acute, if I do say so myself, and—"

I pinched the small of my nose, closed my eyes and shook my head. Computers. Some say you gotta love 'em. I say if you can't boil 'em up and eat 'em with a delicate Bearnaise sauce, they're good target practice.

". . . eh . . . Dave?"

"Yeah, Swishy?"

"Okay to open the air-lock now?" Simultaneously, as he spoke, the air-lock phlooped open.

Oh, my—Geez! I'm not gonna get a chance to capish Swishy! I immediately held my breath— not easy when one's not even *taken* a breath to hold—and set to wondering which orifice would betray me first by bursting under pressure. I felt it might be my shortest 'wondering' in the whole of my thirty-two years.

My cheeks bulged red with the effects of my frantic, and frankly futile, 'avoiding certain death' struggle. Suddenly I noticed a breeze waft over my close-to-bursting cheeks, and I released my captive breath (which, I've got to admit was a touch funky—no toothbrush since dear old Mother Earth) and I noticed, quite oddly, I *wasn't* dead.

Oh, what the hell, it's a good day to die. Taking in a great drought of air in one swoop, I found it fresh and little on the minty side. Seems like I'd landed—*been thrown out on my ass*—on Planet Mentos.

"Man, you are a lucky, lucky Swishy," I said, patting the computer module. "And someday—I'll use your remaining parts as one elaborate Tinker-Toy."

I'd just finished ruffling Swishy's hair—so to speak—when a soft rapping sounded outside the air-lock door. "Who knew I was dropping in?" I wondered aloud. I drew my gun and stealthily made my way to the open door, where I did my best James Bond imitation. My gun barrel preceded my nose around the door's edge and it pointed at a strange purplish-pink and blue creature with one eye.

"What the—" I greeted the space oddity in my best Earth Ambassador manner.

It reached up a purplish-pink and blue tentacle and said one word as it touched my nose: "Bloop."

Uni-Houston? The Feagle has landed.

I thought the tentacled jellyish-thing was smiling, at least things and tiny mounds of Jello moved around its face kinda like there was a frat party going on. Still that didn't give me pause to shoot it. I'd ask questions later.

"Eat shit and die—alien scum!" I screamed as I pulled the trigger. The gun in my hand failed to buck, like it did in training. Instead, it did a comical imitation of my new found friend. As a tiny white flag deployed from the barrel, the finely calibrated weapon said: "Bloop." That, and it waved the tiny flag in the minty breeze, bearing the message written in Uni-NASA font: "Gotcha, Dumbass." Uni-NASA. They're all a bunch of chimps. Chimps with brain farts.

My new friend—this brutha from anutha mutha—smiled again. I thought. Then he raised his tentacle once more, touched my nose and said: "Bloop." Like what the hell else was he *gonna* say? He had 'Bloop' down pat and for him, it worked.

Again I pinched the small of my nose. Raising my head, I smiled. "Welcome to the Feagle," I offered wearily. "I'm Dave. And over in the corner—Swishy takes requests."

"Bloop," he said in response to my friendly greeting.

"Ahhh . . . and *you* must be Bloop."

I'd taken a folding lawn chair (See? The Uni-NASA chimps *had* thought of me) outside onto the Feagle's purplish lawn. I also carted out a six pack of Jägermeister and a big bag of pork rinds. Hell, I was here, might as well make the best of it, right? Bloop flow-walked at my heels. I just couldn't shake the little guy, and frankly, I was growing a tad fond of the wobbly grape-ish-Jello-looking creature.

My dogs were barking as I plopped down on the recliner, and I laid back and put my feet up. *Ya know? Maybe it won't be too bad here on Planet Mentos,* I thought. *After all, I got enough Jäger to last for a few years, pork rinds out the wazoo... and good ole Bloop here to keep me company. Sure the conversation'll surely lag from time to time— but the little guy's no Swishy. An' thank the Jäger-gods for that.*

As if he'd read my mind, Bloop dipped his tentacle into my beer—after asking a polite: "Bloop" first.

"So, little guy," I grinned, "what'cha think of the Jäger, *Buddie?*" I did my best Pauly Shore's 'Weasel' imitation. Bloop's multi-hued bloopy skin—for want of a better word—swirled like a kaleidoscope. I wondered if this response meant he liked it or if I was about to see Jello 'call Ralph' like a greeny freshman.

Suddenly, as if in answer to my good-natured question, Bloop reached up and stuck his Jäger-lubed tentacle in my right ear.

"*Bloooop!!!*" he shrilled.

"Wwhaxafraxal!!!" I shrieked. Okay . . . what *is* the proper response to an over-amorous alien who's just made your ear his bitch? I thought 'Wwhaxafraxal' perfectly represented my thoughts of the moment.

He probed my ear like he was mining for gold. Was it enjoyable? Bout as fun as a deep colonoscopy by Jäger-drenched spongy Jello on a stick. Don't know why, but as the Jello-probing tentacle plunged deeper, my eyes rolled back in my head, and—I swear—I *saw* England. And the Queen. Wow. Not that I was enjoying it much, but this rivaled that wild night in Bangkok. I knew I'd never look at grape Jello in the same way again. And in all the chaotic . . . *activity*, Bloop kept up a steady stream of 'Blooping'.

"Bloop-Bloop-Bloop," he sang. "Bloop-Bloop-Thank-The-Twux-That's-Over...." He withdrew the offending tentacle and 'liquefied' slightly into the purplish grass. Guess it was good for him, too.

When I'd recovered from my swoon—okay—I admit it—I swooned—I sat up on the lounge chair, grabbed my Jello-dripping ear and glared at the soggy alien who'd half-melted at my feet. "Hey, man . . . that wasn't the *least bit* cool! You think just 'cause I gave you a sip of my beer you got the right to make advances with my *ear???* Dude, you got anuther think comin' if *you* think I'm gonna stand for *that* kind of behavior! An' anuther thing . . . ." My rant died down, kinda like I'd been pricked like a circus balloon. "*You talked???* You freakin' talked—English? *English???* Am I losing my mind?"

Bloop sighed. "How many times did I have to ask you if you'd mind if I gathered needed information? Does *'please'* not mean anything to your kind? Frankly, human, I'm just not that impressed. I mean, sure, you've proven you've enough intelligence in that rigid body of yours to crash onto my planet, but have you never been debriefed?"

I glared at the English speaking grape Jello. "Why, I never . . . ." I muttered. *"That's* what they call it on Planet Mentos? *Debriefing?* Well, I gottcher debriefing right here, fella!" I starting up out of the lounger, simultaneously grabbing my crotch. Bad move. I slipped on some leftover Jello-lube pooled at my feet and I sprawled back into the lounger.

Have you ever heard the rude laughter of grape Jello? No? Well... it sounds a lot like 'Bloop' mixed with tiny silver bells.

A few hours brought out my amorous Jello's story.

"The name's not Bloop—it's Pwerltaflaganmuxa-Twux. Friends call me Pwerltaflaganmuxa." Then he sighed. "But I'm assuming I'll forever be Bloop to you." He tipped his own icy cold Jägermeister to what passed for lips on Planet Mentos. "I must say, Dave, the taste does grow on one, does it not?"

I gave a thumb's up to my wobbly-bobbly new grapey friend while downing my third beer. Yup. Planet Mentos might not be such a horrible place after all. Good beer. Good eats. I'd just have to keep a sharp eye on the Jello.

Bloop asked, "Bet you're wondering why I knocked on your door, aren't you?"

"Well... the thought did cross my mind. Especially bout the time you stuck your 'information gathering tool' in my right ear."

"Dave, I *said* I was sorry. I had no way of true communication before the debriefing. I had to gain access to your thoughts and knowledge." He shifted his gelatinous mass and burped. The curse of the Jägermeister had claimed another victim. Bloop was drunk on his ass... well, what *passed* for his ass. He'd had only one. Lightweight Twux. The purple Jello just couldn't hold his beer. "You see, Dave... it's a matter of life and death."

"It always is, Bloop, it always is."

"No, no," he protested, waving that offensive tentacle in the air for emphasis, "no—I don't mean like that—I mean . . . it's the Surrggeeons. They'll kill you if you stay here."

I laughed. "You mean to tell me, this planet is inhabited by gangs of murderous doctors? No news to me, Bloop. It's been that way on Earth for years." I laughed again and shooed him back with my hand.

Bloop shook his head. At least, I thought that's what he was doing. He gave the impression of the reaction a grape Jello mold might make with Bill Cosby coming at it with a spoon. "No, Dave. Not surgeons—*SurrggEEons*. The emphasis is on the 'e' sound. They're beautiful people."

"Well . . . don't hate them because they're beautiful, Bloop. The girl can't help it, ya know."

Bloop made a gesture that implied he was pinching the bridge of his nose, if he'd had one. "Good golly, you're dense. Never mind. There's no time. We've got to leave this planet."

"Next you're gonna tell me you've got two tickets to Clarksville and you'll meet me at the station. We'll have time for coffee kisses and—"

"*Will you just shut up—you moron???*"

You've never been yelled at until you've had a slap-down from grapey Jello. He glared at me (as well as Jello can glare) from his sprawling place on the purple grass. A few seconds passed while I digested Bloop's anger. "Okay. You've got my attention—you've got the floor. Why, Oh Great Bloop, should I be afraid of a bunch of beautiful surgeons?"

"SurrggEEons."

I rolled my eyes. "SurrggEEons."

"Well, for one thing, they love their drink." He said this and shifted his weight again. It seemed Bloop wasn't that comfortable on the purple grass.

"So what? I've got a butt-load of Jägermeister in my storage, and surely they'll supply some eats, if I'm a good boy and say *pleeease*." I batted my eyes, coyly.

"Gag me," Bloop moaned. "Simple, simple human. How can I get you to see, when I say 'they love their drink', I'm talking about you and me."

I gulped. "Ya . . . ya . . . ." I gulped again. "You and ma . . . ma . . . me?"

"I'm thinking you've just had a light bulb moment, right?" Bloop smiled and it wasn't as attractive a sight as one might have imagined. "So, *Kirk*. It's time you started thinking about getting our asses off my lovely planet."

I shook my head and was rewarded by a dizzy spell. Enough with the beer, already—this was getting serious. "But . . . I can't," I wailed. "I was dumped on this Purple Hazed Planet with no fuel—no way back!" I felt I was close to tears. *Man up, Feagle!* I silently commanded myself.

"That's where I come in." To say the grapey Jello looked smug would be an understatement.

"You?" I asked, "What can you do? I mean, no offence, but on my planet, you're a chilled sweet treat."

Bloop shot me a look that could kill. "That's disgusting. And might I add: *Eeeew!* Get serious, Dave. You've got to get off this planet just as much as I do. If those Surrggeeons catch scent of your blood... let's just say, there'll be a little less Dave to go around. I have a plan."

I looked at his quivering gelatinous mass in front of me. "It wouldn't by any chance be a *clever* plan, would it?" I raised an eyebrow at the purple Jello.

"In fact, it is." And he winked. Again with the less than attractive sight.

Night had fallen like a drunken whore and we'd been busy with Bloop's clever plan. It appeared we'd take my 'space-woody' with it's ample storage in the back and sneak up on the Surrggeeons, so to speak. "You know, don't ya, Uni-NASA didn't intend for the woody to be used as a pack mule?" I waved my arms at the woody for emphasis.

"And your point, Dave? We've *got* to break into their food supply and grab as many canisters as we can. They'll each weigh about fifty of your Earth pounds—I don't think you'll want to lug them back here on your own."

How could I argue with that logic. "Okay, Mr. Spock. Let's get these doggies rollin'! Move `em out—Rawhide!"

Bloop sneered, "You're just a mish-mash of arcane television barf-up, aren't you?"

"*Oh, yeah?* Well, you're purple and sticky and your mother

dresses you funny—so there!"

We'd been on the 'trail' for about thirty minutes, bouncing around in the space-woody, when I finally broke the silence. "So... this stuff in the canisters . . . you can use it to power my craft back into space? Power it all the way back to Earth?"

"Yes."

"And what do *you* get out of it, Bloop?"

"In your culture-speak, I'll get a ticket to ride. Like I told you, I too must abandon my planet."

I grinned. "So, say it, Bloop. Give it up. Come on!"

The blob of grape Jello sighed. Then he snarled, "Okay. I need you, Dave. I *need* you to get me off this planet before I'm mixed in a Surrggeeon's cocktail. Okay? You proud of yourself you've made me beg?" He turned his grapey face to the window and gazed out at his planet's three moons.

We traveled in silence for a few Earth miles. Finally, I spoke. "Sorry. Man, I don't know what got into me. Here I'm a visitor to your world, you befriend me—in a rather sticky and disgusting way, I might add—but what the hey—and then you offer to save my life. I'm sorry I ragged you, man. We cool?"

Bloop turned from his window-brooding. "Yeah . . . we're cool. You're gonna wanna take a left up the road after that big boulder. And kill the lights. The Surrggeeon's warehouse will be in sight soon. We do just what I told you back at your craft."

"Roger."

"You know? I'd just as soon you call me Bloop. It's grown on me. Kinda like that furry stuff on top of your pointy head."

I grinned and slapped the woody into fifth gear. "*Bu*-ddie!" I crowed.

It was completely dark when we arrived at the warehouse. No lights protected the unfenced building.

"What do they need lights for?" Bloop said. "They're the hunters on this planet. They have no fear of my kind... never did."

Suddenly serious, I asked, "What did the Surrggeeons *do* to your people, Bloop? Tell me."

He sighed. "Dave? That story will have to wait for another time. Perhaps when we're safely away. For now, time is precious. Let's roll."

We entered the food supply warehouse by a back door. It was unguarded. The Surrggeeons *really* had no fear of Jello-blobbed terrorists. Guess when you're the Doberman, a tiny Chihuahua is a mere nuisance. Dim overhead lights showed rows and rows of silver canisters, about the size of a scuba diver's tank.

"What's in the cans, Bloop?"

"Our fuel," was his only answer.

We'd nearly loaded the woody full—and Bloop had underestimated the weight—more like *eighty* pounds each—when lights went on at the front of the warehouse. I saw my first Surrggeeon. My, he was beautiful. He'd have put that old-time movie star, George Clooney, to shame. My mind was growing 'Clooney-Moony' as I gazed at him—don't get me wrong—I'm the straightest guy you'd ever meet—but that Surrggeeon was the most beautiful *man* I'd ever seen. It was like I wanted to . . . lick his face. In fact, I'd taken a step toward him, close to the shadow's edge, when Bloop slapped me across the face with his tentacle.

I snarled and grabbed my cheek. "Ow! That hurt—you little sumbitc—"

"Thank me later," Bloop hissed. "You're just had your first Surrggeeon mesmerizing. Feels good, but doesn't end pleasant. Let's get the last of these canisters in the woody and make like a bush and leave."

"That's make like a tree and leaf, by the way."

"Whatever," said my Jello companion in crime.

All at once, an alarm sounded and the whole warehouse was bathed in bright light. A dozen Surrggeeon heads turned in our direction and they sniffed the air.

"They've got our scent," Bloop cried, "Run!"

We ran. We ran like bloodthirsty Surrggeeons were on our tail— which they were.

After slamming the door on the nearly full woody, we leaped

into the seats (Bloop managed a kind of jiggly leap) and we got our asses out of Dodge. I put the pedal to the metal and hauled ass down the road—reaching speeds of thirty-five miles an hour, easy.

"Check our back, Bloop!" I cried, "Are they following us?"

"Relax, but don't slow down, Dave. They'll be on foot. They have little need of mechanical conveyances." He shook his head. "That's one of the things that makes the Surrggeeon so dangerous. One rarely knows death has come, because it arrives on silent feet." He sounded sad and weary.

I felt the anguish of the small blob of purple Jello . . . what I mean to say is, I could feel my *friend's* pain as we sped toward my landing module. And although I thought I knew the answer to my question, I asked it anyway. Softly. "Bloop? Please tell me what happened to your people. What did the Surrggeeon do to the . . . the . . . ."

"The Twux?" he finished for me. "It's a long story, really. Let me shorten it for you, for now. Dave? I'm the last of the Twux."

I whispered, "The last? You mean, there are no more Twux? No more?"

"Bingo."

We sat in silence for a mile or more, while I digested Bloop's revelation. No more Twux. Bloop was the last of his kind. How would *I* have faced being the last man on Earth? Not as well as my friend Bloop, I wagered.

Finally I spoke, whispering, "Bummer, dude."

"You got that right."

Suddenly I was filled with a new anger at the Surrggeeon. Who were *they* to decide a whole race of beings should be wiped off their planet? Even if it did smell like a tasty breath mint? "I've a good mind to turn this buggy around and go back and kick some Surrggeeon's butt!!!" I yelled into the woody's cab.

"Please don't, Dave." Bloop spoke as if he had the weight of his minty planet on his gelatinous shoulders. "You'd not have a chance to honor the brave Twuxes who've gone on before. The Surrggeeons would make a sport of killing you—they'd pass you around until you were drained and weeping for death. It's not pretty." He leaned his stubby gelatin-like neck back against the headrest and sighed. "The

Surrggeeons *are* beautiful, certainly, but the death they hand out isn't. Let's just get back to your ship, okay?"

"You got it, Bloop." I shook my head at the injustice and murmured, "You've got it, *Bu*-ddie."

We'd been back at my landing craft for a good thirty minutes and had nearly poured all the silver containers' contents into my fuel tanks. No, it wasn't an easy thing to do—what with the metal containers being so heavy—but somehow knowing an angry mob of Surrggeeons were breathing down our necks served to hurry the task. "That's the next to the last one, Bloop. Maybe you'd better board and find a safe place for blast off? I mean, it wouldn't do for you to—" My advice died in my throat. The Surrggeeon, and their fiery torches crested the hill about a mile away. And they were running. They were so close I could hear their growls. The murderous Surrggeeon had the scent of blood and they'd not be denied.

I hurriedly emptied the last container, spilling about a cupful on my pants. Oh, well. It didn't seem to be caustic. "You belted in, Bloop? We're outta here, *Bu*-ddie!" I ran up the landing ramp, twirled around and slammed a hand on the air-lock door. The sound of its closing 'phloop' was music fit for Broadway . . . . oh, no. . . . *pleeease* don't let him—

Too late. Swishy started off quiet, before building to a crescendo: "What good... is sitting... alone in your room? Come hear the music *plaaay*. Life is... a Cabaret, old chum. Come to the—"

"Oh, *hell* no!" I screamed. "I will *not* listen to Broadway music all the way home—*capish???* Swishy—do I have to come back there and capish your ass to get a little peace and quiet?"

A five second silence brought my answer. "No, Dave. I'm all capished-up back here. Have a nice day."

"I intend to, Swishy, I intend to." I took my seat at the controls, pushed the necessary buttons like a man possessed, and in moments had the engines purring like a kitten—if the kitten had been a sixty ton feline. As our craft left the purple ground, I looked out the cockpit window and watched as the terrible gang of Surrggeeons raged over Feagle's lawn. We'd lifted off none too soon.

We'd barely left the gravity field of Bloop's planet when I glanced down at my stained pants. The spots where the fuel had splattered were a sticky purple. My heart sank. "Bloop," I said, "please tell me what happened to your people?"

"I think you know, Dave." My little grapey purple friend softly said. "I think you know that we're flying to your planet on the wings of brave Twuxes. And we shall honor their name by reaching safety."

As I charted a course home through the starry galaxy, I reflected on Bloop's words. "I think you're gonna like Earth, Bloop. Though it doesn't smell quite as nice as *your* planet."

Alien Universe

Jeannine Baumgartle

Have you noticed
that doorframes are not
as good at dodging
as they used to be?
Tables have more corners, too,
and stairs a steeper grade.
Coins are more slippery
and the floor is farther away.
Wherever I shop,
people avert their eyes
or stare at the lady
damaged by more than age,
and I want to tell them,
—No, I am not
an abused escapee
from a convalescent center.
I have merely left
my space suit
to be dry cleaned.

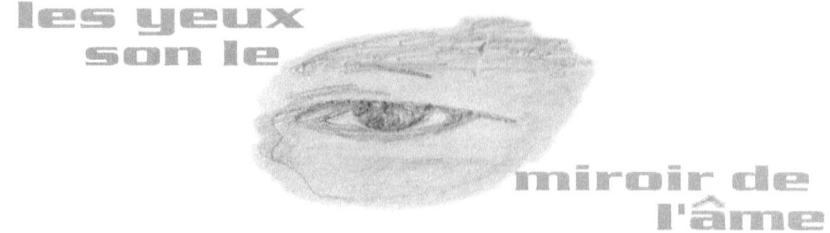

les yeux
son le

miroir de
l'âme

SOLO FOR MULTIPLE INSTRUMENTS

Marian Allen

The solitude was appalling. She had agreed to it, had signed a waiver along with all the other paperwork for Volunteer Pioneers, had trained for a month with all her social circuits muted before leaving Earth, but the reality . . . . How could she have imagined the reality?

Tears overwhelmed Gale's eyes, flowing down her cheeks when she tried to blink them away. The other colonists in the dome's common room went about their business or pleasure, unaware of her distress. *At least,* she thought, *I could stand up and wail, and then they'd know. The people in other parts of the colony wouldn't know even then. I can't tell them. I can't reach them.* She blinked again and wiped her cheeks with her palms. She fumbled in her jumpsuit pocket for a tissue. *Gale Sanderson, cry-baby,* she thought scornfully.

"Hey." Toby Barnes, the Project Facilitator spoke aloud—well, he had to, didn't he? With no social circuits to connect their minds, out loud was the only way to talk. He sat down next to her on the couch, his voice soft and husky, warm and calm. "Just starting to hit you?" He tapped his forehead.

Gale nodded. "It—" The syllable came out thick and rough. She cleared her throat and tried again. "It isn't as if I didn't know ahead of time. I knew. I was okay with it."

"Seemed like a good idea, didn't it, Sanderson?" Toby said. "Get some space for yourself." Toby—he was Dr. Barnes, officially, but said he preferred Toby—greeted every new colonist personally and apparently kept up a protective observation for a while after arrival.

She nodded and dabbed at her nose with her paper tissue, which was now in shreds.

Barnes handed her a handkerchief. "Kind of like asking for a little elbow room and finding yourself alone in the haunted castle."

She blew her nose and laughed uncertainly. "Hardly haunted."

"No?"

"My *brain*? Thanks, boss."

"That's how it hit me, anyway." He leaned forward, forearms resting on his thighs, gaze flicking around the common area. "That's how it still hits me. With the network, you're never alone with your thoughts, unless you want to be. Without the network, it's just you and memory and imagination. All these haunted castles, moving around each other, each one with one living resident looking out, trying to catch a glimpse of another living resident."

If she had still been connected, Gale would have passed that on to her network. Now, nobody would hear it but the two of them. It seemed a shame. It seemed a waste.

"They told me it was because I'd be too far from my network to pick up transmissions. But it seems like they could connect us all in a new network—just us in the colony. It would cost something to reconfigure everybody's software, but still . . . ."

"False economy," Toby said. "You're right. Keeping us in a network would be cheaper than mental health counseling to keep us from going buggy."

"Does the counseling help?"

The Facilitator looked at her over his shoulder and rolled his eyes around and around. "Why do you ask?"

She cackled. "Do it again," she said, and tapped the center of her left palm three times with a fingernail.

Toby looked away, so he didn't see her face when she remembered her *video on* signal wasn't going to work.

The planet had not been Terraformed. There had been talk of it, but sentimentalists and budget-watchers had united against it. Instead, there were what they called "containments": geodesic domes like blisters on the surface, connected by tunnels dug underground. They had brought anything they couldn't produce for themselves, and supply ships would bring more once a year.

"If we're still here in another year," Anouk Barronne said cheerfully.

After three days on site, Gale still automatically checked her useless social circuits for the emoticons that would tell her if Anouk were serious or joking.

She and Anouk, each tri-lingual in French, English and Esperanto, were on assignment in one of the culinary herb gardens.

The bunny slopes—as the staff called the domes where the neophyte Volunteers worked—had opaque shielding, the lighting entirely artificial. Newcomers to the colonies often felt threatened by a clear view of the alien landscape. Less often, they felt drawn to it, and some had been known to open a hatch and step out, in spite of unbreatheable air and unknowable pathogens.

"What do you mean, 'If we're here in another year'?" Gale checked the commissary order and broke off some dill fronds. The bright, thick scent almost made her giddy. Even after she sealed the harvest into a freshbag, the air and her hands were redolent with the herb's clear note.

"Because of the—What do you call them?" Anouk cocked her head, then grimaced.

With a not-entirely-compassionate pang of empathy, Gale realized Anouk had been trying to access a French/English dictionary site that wasn't available to her anymore.

Anouk frowned briefly, then said, "Gremlins. We have gremlins."

Does she even know what that means? Gale smiled at the secret freedom of thinking what she wanted as directly as she wanted. No checking to make sure she was thinking off-line, no worrying that she might have been hacked, her stream of consciousness broadcast on rogueband. It was this freedom, dimly dreamt, that had nudged her toward the Volunteer Pioneer program in the first place.

Anouk misinterpreted her smile. "It's true. Ever since construction started. Tools missing, equipment scratched and dented overnight, food contaminated. Once, a storage bin was found forced open and an atmo suit had been taken out of it and turned inside out. What do you say to that?"

"Sounds like somebody has a sophomoric sense of humor."

"Huh!" Anouk made one of her vast repertoire of unattractive sounds. "No one would contaminate food in space. Not for a joke."

"Sabotage, then."

The Frenchwoman gave an eloquent shrug—something no emoticon could ever fully convey. "They say it was gremlins. They say we still have them. The ones who have been here the longest, they say it."

"They're just trying to intimidate us." Gale stopped working and stared at the skin of the dome, as if she could see through the shielding. "They're telling scary stories to the new kids."

"Perhaps," Anouk agreed, her voice implying that she didn't agree but didn't want to argue.

Gale shivered. It was, possibly, the most disconcerting thing about being off the network: having to pay such intimate attention to non-verbal communication with mere acquaintances and even strangers. No, worse was the feeling that other people were paying that kind of close attention to you.

Anouk had gone to use the "water box", as she insisted on calling it, and to bring them an afternoon snack. Gale worked her way toward the end of the row, trimming and packing dill for the commissary.

The closer she came to the dome surface, the stronger the feeling of being watched became. Her own reflection startled her, the apprehensive eyes so much wider than usual, the features blurred by the panel's semi-matte finish, colors leeched by the dull silver tint. *It's only me.* Gale met her own hazy gaze in the gray panel. *Or is it?*

She stared at her image on the thin barrier between the inside and the outside, at herself-that-was-not-herself, and her heart pounded, reveling in the presence of another consciousness.

"Hello," she said, suddenly fiercely curious about this new acquaintance. "Pleased to meet you. I would offer to trade profile locations with you, but that's a thing of the past, isn't it?"

"Ah, Dieu!" Anouk called from the doorway. "Don't start talking to yourself, my friend. That way lies madness." She handed Gale a thermal glass sipping mug of black coffee and a freshbag of three ginger snaps.

Embarrassed, Gale said, "I wasn't talking to myself. I was talking to the gremlins."

"I see." Anouk nodded and took a careful sip of the hot coffee. "Now, does that make you less mad, or more mad? And will you tell Toby Barnes, or do I have to . . . What is the phrase? 'rat you out'?"

"Tell Toby? Why?" But she knew why. Anouk didn't even bother to answer. They couldn't afford to have anybody go off the rails in a pioneer site. One lunatic in a closed environment with such a limited population, so few of whom were expendable, could be a disaster. "Projecting oneself as a separate entity" was one of the things the counselor had specifically warned them about. Any instance—any suspected instance—was to be reported to one of the mental health staff or the Project Facilitator. She wasn't certain that one creepy moment meant her brains were scrambled, but nobody could afford to take that chance. She would have to tell Toby.

The counseling session was a little more crowded than she had expected. Doctors Paulo Battaglia (psychologist) and Folame Simisola (psychiatrist) were both present, which wasn't entirely surprising. Toby was there, too, which she hadn't anticipated, sitting behind her line of sight as if he were just a fly on the wall.

It made her nervous. The whole thing made her nervous.

Dr. Battaglia smiled reassuringly. "You aren't in trouble, you know, Ms. Sanderson," he said. "In fact, it speaks very well for your stability, that you reported this immediately. I hope that helps."

It did, actually. She relaxed.

"You say you felt you were meeting someone new?"

"I didn't look like myself. The reflection was . . ." she held her hand up in front of her face and wiggled her fingers, "distorted. I guess that was the thing."

"It's very difficult," Dr. Simisola said, her voice smooth and kind, "and more difficult for some than for others, to lose the network. Some people feel . . . lonely, inside their own heads. Some of them . . . ." She trailed off and waved a pink-palmed hand at Dr. Battaglia. "Continue, please, doctor."

He nodded his appreciation, still smiling at Gale. "Did you fantasize any words? Actual words?"

Had she? It almost seemed she had, but . . . . "No, I don't think so. I think it was more of an impression. It *was* like the network. It was like somebody new popping up in your stream, you know? Like when you have the MagNet engaged, and you and somebody within each other's compatibility parameters come within six degrees of each other and *pop*—you're in chat together. It was like that. You know: There you are, and 'hello' is just a formality."

Dr. Battaglia's smile widened to show he understood. "How did you feel about that?"

"Surprised. Excited. Happy." She huffed a mirthless laugh. "Then stupid."

"No, no, no," Dr. Simisola protested gently, patting the arm of her chair in lieu of Gale's out-of-reach hand.

"No reason to feel negative about the experience," Dr. Battaglia agreed. "It isn't uncommon. Many people—especially new arrivals—experience what we call a phantom network. With a phantom network, patients report a sense of a presence or presences inside the mind or body, thoughts not their own and not representing themselves as their own, sometimes actual words or phrases or whole conversations, usually with people they had known on the disconnected circuits."

"No, it was nothing like that. It was like meeting somebody *new*. Is that worse?"

Dr. Battaglia spread his hands. "No, indeed. You have nothing to worry about, young woman."

Dr. Simisola glanced over Gale's shoulder for the first time during the interview, to where Gale had heard Toby seat himself. "I tend to agree. Medication is not indicated."

Dr. Battaglia tapped the arm of his chair with a fingernail. "Counseling..." he mused aloud. "Isolation."

"Isolation?" Gale sat forward in alarm. "What?"

"Just for a week or so. With counseling every day. Just until we're sure this is resolved."

"But . . . . Isolation?" Her breath nearly stopped, just thinking about it.

"Phantom network syndrome has proved highly contagious and highly disruptive, as you can imagine." Dr. Battaglia folded his hands across his stomach and leaned back, at ease and comforting. "You won't be entirely secluded, of course, Ms. Sanderson. Dr. Simisola and I will visit you every day; Dr. Barnes—" he nodded at Toby— "will visit you; nurses and orderlies will monitor you and tend to your needs. And, of course, you'll keep busy. I understand your Esperanto and French are quite good?"

At last, something she was sure of. "Yes, sir."

"We'll put you to work double-checking the translations of reports, then. Dry, but challenging. I think you'll find your mind pleasantly occupied, and these disturbing symptoms will just—" he fluttered a hand in the air, "vanish."

For two days, Gale thought he was right. For two days, there wasn't a trace of anything in her head that recalled the wonderfully dear jumble of input she had thought she wanted to escape. She remembered her mother saying, "All those years of taking you three to lessons and practices and games and recitals and friends' houses and what-have-you, I looked forward to having my time to myself. Now you're all grown and gone, I miss it." Empty nest syndrome, she called it. *So what do I have—Empty head syndrome?*

From time to time, she felt herself under observation, but she had been told she would be, and she soon learned to ignore it.

For two days, she sat, with her back to the opaque dome, reading brief reports—essays, really—on basic scientific principles. The holographic monitor displayed three screens side-by-side, with the same report in English, Esperanto and French, and she was to read each one and mark any translation mistakes. There never were any.

It was obviously busywork, given to her to keep her mind occupied. It didn't matter whether she did it or not, but she did it.

On the third day, came the attack, for want of a better word.

She was jolted upright by a shock of pure joy and triumph. The sense of a lost friend found again was so strong, she bounced in her chair and thought, *U, u, u, u, u! Where u bin? Missed! Missed! And look! I see!* The ghost of another mind—only one, but more than just her own—tumbled around hers like a puppy—poured out happiness and excitement and thoughts she couldn't grasp, as if they were being sent in a language she didn't understand and had never heard before.

"Help," she whispered. Then, louder, she cried, "Help! Dr. Battaglia! Dr. Simisola! Toby! Help me!"

The "other mind" drew back, sending waves of calm. Her terror subsided as the doctors strode into the room, and she wept because she was ill, alone in her haunted castle.

"Don't worry, Sanderson." Toby had come down to her quarters to keep her company and distract her with an evening of chess. Neither one knew more than the basic moves, so they were evenly matched. "A lot of people have trouble adjusting. You get used to it. If you don't, what's the worst thing that can happen?"

"I go crazy."

Toby bounced a fragment of cookie off her forehead and spoke the sound effect: "*Doink!* No. Wrong. The docs wouldn't let you go crazy. They'll get you through this. Worst case: They hold you steady till the supply ship comes back, and ship you back to civilization. Some people just aren't cut out for this life, Sanderson. No shame."

She rested her head in her hand, her elbow on the table, and moved a pawn at random. "I don't understand why I can't just stay down here all the time. I never had any of those 'episodes' until I started working topside."

He frowned at the board. Without looking up, he asked, in a flat tone, "Was it really that bad?"

"No." Numb with desolation, she said, "It was great. Like a mirage in the desert. Looks like life, but there's nothing there." She watched Toby make a move, and said, not caring, "I think you won."

The next day, they gave her anti-anxiety drugs. Dr. Simisola dispensed the tablet in person, along with a sympathetic smile.

"Will this stop it happening?" Gale asked.

"Perhaps, or perhaps not. But it will mute the fright and distress if something *should* happen. We want you to open another holo-screen on your desk. If you have a recurrence of this conviction that you're being invaded, we want you to journal it." After a brief hesitation, she continued, "If you can. If you can't—if your thoughts are too chaotic to grasp, or if you begin to feel overwhelmed—call out, as you did yesterday. All right?"

***

Half-way through the day, she was given a set of essays she had seen before. The next set was a repetition, too—same text, same illustrations. As if the task hadn't been boring enough to begin with.

Nevertheless, the drug made her feel too dull to resent the brutal pointlessness of the assignment, and she plodded through the text again, in English, in Esperanto, in French. English, Esperanto, French.

It was working. The medication and the tedium made a perfect team. From the moment she sat down, she had that sense of being in company, but the feeling was muted. She was able to ignore it most of the time. There was an occasional spike of intense happiness but, by the end of the day, when she could retreat to her quarters, she had experienced nothing to log.

She dreamed of her work. The number of screens open in the air at eye-level changed. Sometimes there were three, sometimes four, sometimes five. When she tried to count them, to hold the number steady, she woke up. The dull dream of a dull mind worn out by a dull job.

"Today," Dr. Battaglia said in Gale's morning session with the doctors, "I would like for you to journal. Begin with your dreams of last night. And . . . ." He settled himself back in his chair, like a smiley-face emoticon taking any sting out of his words, "You meant it for the best, but you should have logged those bursts of emotion."

"I thought I was supposed to be ignoring them."

"We're seeing if we can't disconnect the phantom network. As long as you sense connections to other people, as if your social circuits were still active, we need to be aware of it." His warm smile drew one from her.

Dr. Simisola said, "It's true that the essays you're being sent are repeating. We'd like you to continue to read them through as usual, but if you get too bored to read consciously, feel free to journal spontaneously. Anything that comes into your mind. If you can separate and label the thoughts you recognize as your own and the ones you've assigned to this 'other', that would be particularly helpful."

She managed to get through most of the next day with no trouble. Although she had no place to post it and nobody to read it,

Gale had continued to keep a journal after she entered the program. She called it onto the fourth screen and, in between sets of essays (Newton's Laws, Relativity Simplified, Refraction of Light), she dipped in and out of old entries.

Toby said it was like being alone in a haunted castle. Gale read the journal entry and shivered.

She paged past everything that had happened since the initial onset of the syndrome. When she reached the current date, she inserted a holographic video she'd made of herself as a baby morphing into herself now, ending with the hologram she used as her virtual reality avatar. She reviewed the VR training program she had used before she decided to join the Volunteers, showing the planet from space, the landing pod sinking closer to the surface, seeing the domes from above, then from the ground. She watched her avatar board the shuttle, then saw, through her avatar's eyes, the off-kilter colors and shapes of the local landscape and foliage, which only looked like Terran colors and shapes because those were all she had as reference. Here, she inserted holograms of landscapes she knew, personally or through pictures.

The virtual shuttle entered the airlock dome and, after fast-forwarding through decontamination and atmosphere/pressure "normalization"—meaning, of course, Earth-normal—Gale's avatar shook hands with a smiling Toby Barnes and exchanged greetings and introductions.

She played that part three times.

"Hi!" Toby said, over and over. "Happy to have you here."

The program malfunctioned at that point, and she couldn't follow herself through the underground corridors, or access maps or blueprints of the facility.

She checked other maps and holograms of the planet, and they came up with no problem. She pulled up one of the exterior of Dome 16a, section 3, ward 7, cubicle 12, and found she could do a cut-away view. There was her avatar, sitting at the desk, working away. She rotated the perspective to watch her own face as she watched her avatar watch her avatar watching her avatar.

She watched herself smile, then she jumped as the program replayed her first handshake with the Program Facilitator.

Gremlins, she thought. *Here's one for Anouk's collection.*

Curious, she looked up "gremlins" in the mainframe dictionary. "Imaginary beings playfully blamed for causing mechanical malfunctions or bad luck."

The "other mind", which she had been not-quite-sure was lurking around, de-lurked.

Gale changed the font in her journal and typed, *I am not gremlins. The castle is not haunted. Hi. Happy to have you here. Snoopy dancing.*

"Help?" she said. "Help help help help help?"

She typed, **Who are you?**

There was a swirl of static in her mind, sounds and visualizations she couldn't understand or interpret.

The door opened and Toby and both doctors eased in. Gale, borne along on a wave of delight, said, "Hi. Happy to have you here. I'm not crazy, and you know it."

Her fingers itched and she typed what came into her head:
Sound record. Please. Relax.

She switched on the audio and closed her eyes.

The sounds she made weren't singing and weren't talking; she just made whatever sounds she felt compelled to make by the presence in her head. Some intelligible words from the scientific essay on her screens came out, but most of the vocal stream was just noise.

When she seemed to be finished, she opened her eyes and told her observers, "That wasn't me, by the way."

She clicked to the next set of essays, said, "That was *Elementary Principles of Optics*, by Dr. Prandash Gupta. For my next selection, I'm going to do a little piece called *Thermodynamics*, by Dr. Bailey Dwyer, and it goes something like this."

At the end of the translation, her throat was scratchy and her voice was hoarse.

She was also at home with the entity visiting her. She smiled blandly at the doctors who waited breathlessly for what she would do next, letting them wait while she and her new friend held a private conversation.

I can't do any more today. I'll see you tomorrow.
You aren't freaked? You know I'm friending you?
I know. Thank you.

Thank you back.

She stood up and took three dizzy steps toward the door. Toby pushed between the other doctors and picked her up.

"You rat," she said.

"Phantom network syndrome is a very real condition," Dr. Battaglia insisted, pouring the four of them a second round of champagne.

"But I don't have it," Gale said, inhibitions loosened by the day and the bubbly.

"Ah," said Dr. Simisola, raising a manicured finger, "but we didn't know that. We could only hope."

Apparently, Gale's inhibitions weren't the only ones with their lids coming off. Dr. Battaglia gave his colleague a slight frown and a miniscule head-shake, then turned a bright smile on Gale.

They could only hope.

"That's why you disconnected our social circuits and didn't wire us all together here. You didn't want anything to get in the way of.... Of what?"

"Interspecies communication," Toby said. "This planet looked empty of animal life, but.... Well, you've seen it. It's obviously just impinging on our visual acuity. Instruments built to increase our range of perception picked up shadows and echoes—enough to tell us there was certainly something here. But that didn't help us make contact."

"You needed a filter."

Dr. Battaglia sipped his champagne. "We needed a machine. This machine needed to be sensitive enough to pick up mental emanations, tough enough to stand the stress of sudden input, flexible enough to identify a wide range of possible inputs as significant, precise enough to tune in to the elements of significant input that it could work with and powerful enough to learn almost instantly. Fortunately, such a machine already exists."

"My *brain*? *My* brain?"

"Two brains," said Dr. Simisola. "One on our side, and one on theirs. The odds were against it ever happening, but—" She raised her glass in a salute to Gale.

Toby said, "Anybody who showed or reported signs of phantom network syndrome was isolated. If they were really suffering from a psychological aberration, we wanted to help them deal with that. If they were getting communications from the indigenous life-forms, we wanted to nurture that."

"Without letting them—say, without letting *me*, for instance—know what you were using them—using, for example, *me*—for."

Blithely, Dr. Battaglia said, "We couldn't risk contaminating the experiment. If we had told you what we wanted—"

Dr. Simisola interrupted, "The human mind is staggering in its ability to create an elaborate construct and externalize it."

"But you made the breakthrough." Toby beamed fondly at her. "Against all the odds, you not only made the breakthrough but were able to embrace it and work it. You don't know how fantastic that is." He poured another round. "What a day! What a day!" He lifted his glass and motioned for the other three to do the same. "Interspecies communication!" he declared.

They all clinked glasses.

Gale clinked with them, making a mental list of all the rude words she could teach her new friend.

She smiled and sipped champagne, snug in the knowledge that none of her superiors had the least idea what she was thinking.

METAMORPHIC SPACE

Ardis Moonlight

Once upon an evening deep, as I lay in dreamy sleep,
Drifting through unusual scenes sometimes alerted by a snore,
I would have dozed more, but came a break, for suddenly I was awake,
Something had jarred me to forsake, forsake the sleep to find the core,
What stopped the dream? A storm? An ache? Or something more?
An unknown sound? Or something more?

Ah, distinctly, I remember, this all happened last November
When I left my warming bed to check and cautiously explore,
Pressed a lamp switch for some light—it didn't work, I had no fright,
No light caused by a night wind's might, the wind's might—no bolting
the door,
The unknown sound that woke my resting was the wind—I did
implore—
The force of wind, and nothing more.

To the window surely certain, I pulled back the darkened curtain,
Yet what I saw amazed me, dazed me, never having seen before,
For within my spacious sight, stars and comets filled the night,
Flashing, sparkling, all so bright, so bright, yet there was something
more,
The galaxy through which I flew—but what? But how? What was the
score?
I shuddered, frightened to my core.

Taking in this immense glory, dazzled by novas, planets blurry,
(My spectacles still by the bed—I didn't know I'd have this chore),
Retrieved my glasses, now babbling, for other homes I saw were
traveling,
Following mine, not unraveling, unraveling—there was much more,
Flying through an endless space, this was no dream, this night galore,
I sat in thought, and nothing more.

53

FUTURE PERFECT (TENSE in SPACE)

How long this caravan went through, time had vanished, this I knew,
No moon nor sun to measure hours, that seems now a misplaced lore,
The dark and stars were only showing, and then reduced to two suns
glowing,
Four moons whirling, fields for sowing, sowing strange seeds, maybe
more,
A great sea with large beetles rowing, and mantises not unlike before,
An insect world? Then nothing more.

Night sounds reminded me of frogs, spring peepers at their ponds and
bogs,
And stars, such stars that are so close, the moons of orange pass o'er
the door,
I live alone with neighbors near, each is different on this sphere,
Yet we convey our thoughts and hear, can hear what's said in mindful
pour,
I have begun to hold them dear, and value each new friend and more,
Amidst this gradual change and more.
We're oddities for them to study, growing gardens, our faces ruddy,
Tending with our claws or pinchers the eggs on stalks along the shore.
Sometimes visitors, always unseen, pierce my multiple sun-lit dreams
Of feeding in the purple streams, streams that flow for evermore,
With lithe larvae in the swimming, and me feeding in water's pour,
Now it's this, and something more.

Thumbing books from my cases, I've lost the past in all its traces,
Yet drawn am I to photos of the damselfly, the beauty there—ah, so
much more,
As I explore this boggy land, inoculated, thin and grand,
Drift near orange ferns and rosy sand, rosy sand on the swampy moor,
Lift long, blue transparent wings, then dart with ease above a shore,
Complete am I, for evermore.

SOUL SPEAK

Glenda Mills

Your world and mine have crossed before. It happened about 400 Earth years ago, a couple of generations past for us Adians. It was the time of the Great Viral Plague on Adia and we were in danger of extinction. My grandfather had just been promoted to a harvester in Biolab. We had discovered a way to make a vaccine against the deadly virus. The cure for us lay in the RNA of human embryos – embryos that your government readily sold to ours. When my grandfather entered Biolab on his first day to begin harvesting the RNA, hope was on the horizon, rising like the Twin Stars of Istman at new-day.

I never imagined I would find myself in this position. Before me, in a tiny glass tank, lay the fate of my species. I gently lifted the tissue from its chemical bath and placed it under a microscope. I attached the probe to the suction unit, mindful that both were, by nature of their size and sensitivity, the most fragile equipment I had every operated. I fixed the tissue in my field of vision, and, with the lightest of touches, placed the probe to the organism's side. I was sharpening my focus, looking for the embryo's spine and brain. Once the organic material was suctioned, tubing would carry it to the separator where the precious RNA would be removed.

"Hello?"

The voice was quiet, but very clear and distinct. I looked around me, but there was no one else in the lab. I dismissed the event and returned to my work.

"Hello? Is someone there?"

I looked around again. There was no one vis-

ible. Still, I found it difficult to dismiss the voice a second time. I decided to gather needed data. "Who is speaking?"

"I don't know my name. I don't think I've been given one, yet. Do you have a name?" It was the same voice. My auditory sensors confirmed it.

"My name is Tulin. Where are you? I am receiving auditory stimulation but no visual data."

"I'm afraid I don't know that, either. I was floating in a nice, warm liquid, but now I am laying on something rather cold and hard. I must admit it is not as pleasant. Could you possibly put me back where I was?"

I found it impossible to comply. My appendages were shaking too badly.

"Excuse me, but are you the one who touched my side a moment ago?" the voice inquired. "It tickled."

"My auditory sensors are giving me corrupt data," I said, articulating my perceptions as calmly as I could, given my apparent lapse of reason. "It is the intense stimulation of the new assignment. I am sure that is all. I will exit Biolab, have my mid-day nourishment, and come back to silent tissue."

I knew the embryo could not remain out of the solution while I went for nourishment. I put the probe down as gently as I could, considering my appendages were still unsteady, and slid the tissue mass back into the tiny glass tank. As I was walking away, I heard the voice again.

"Ahh. That's much better. Tell me, Tulin. Are you The Creator?"

I hardly noticed my nourishment. All I could think about was Biolab and the voice. I had heard voices all my existence. When I was young, I had inquired about them. My maternal parent had assured me there was no validity to my sensory perceptions. She had me tested for neurological and psychological defects. None were found. Occasionally, like today, I would still hear something, but I knew there was no logical reason to accept it as reality. As I continued to ponder my young existence, I remembered something—a verbal exchange I had overheard between my maternal and paternal parent.

"He has the gift," my paternal parent had said.

"That is impossible. There has not been an Adian soul speaker for generations."

"I want to send him to the holy ones at Olnon. They can conduct an evaluation and find out if he is hearing the voices of the souls around him," the paternal voice pleaded. It seemed this was not the first time he had made this request.

"I will not have him singled out from the rest of us. If he does have the gift, it is best that he never know. You have heard the rumors. The Powerful Ones do not accept such diversity. He would be taken from us. Is that a consequence you are prepared to endure?" My maternal parent hummed quietly, the sound of deep sadness, a sound I had never heard her make before.

For many minutes, my paternal parent did not speak. I could hear him humming, too. As I listened to their grief, I knew I would not be going to Olnon. "We will not discuss this further," he said at last.

Existence went on after that, and soon I learned to ignore the voices. As with any ability that is not encouraged, my gift for hearing voices lessened. It had been at least a quarter of a generation since I had experienced soul speak.

As I walked back to Biolab, I allowed the data from the first-of-day to engage my thought processes. There were a number of facts that required consideration. If the embryo had a soul, which I now believed to be a reliable conclusion, it was against Adian law to destroy it. This realization led to more undesirable facts. It would be very difficult to convince The Powerful Ones of the truth. When I reported my findings, They would know it was soul speak. I had learned during my existence that my parents' previous concerns were valid. Accepting the truth would also mean abandoning the best hope Adia had for survival. The embryo's question resounded again and again in my cranial cavity. "Tulin, are you The Creator?" No, I was not The Creator, but with each passing moment of time, I became more and more resolved that I would not be the destroyer, either. I modified my course to arrive at a new destination.

A dome of electromagnetic energy protected The Edifice of

The Powerful Ones, giving the outward appearance that the building was unguarded. The outer walls were constructed with mud from the Wurn Plains. With a deep intake of atmosphere, I approached the vibrating energy field, placed a trembling appendage against it, and spoke my identification number. The vibration ceased and I crossed the threshold onto the grounds.

Once inside The Edifice, I was escorted to a large, bare room. In the center was a single stone bench. I was told to sit and wait. It is true that the passage of time is distorted when a person is in an unpleasant or painful situation. The actual number of moments that passed on the time dial was disproportional to the estimations in my cranial cavity.

When The Powerful Ones entered the room, I lowered my head, keeping my visual sensors focused on the floor. It would have been a gesture of punishable disrespect to look upon Their countenances.

"2311-078-8489, do you have need to address The Powerful Ones concerning a matter of grave importance?"

"I do."

"Speak. We are willing to listen."

Vocalizing two short words had been a challenge. I swallowed, hoping I could relieve the tension that was strangling me from inside. I had much to articulate. "I am Tulin, a harvester in Biolab. First-of-day, I reported there to begin my duties. I heard a voice speaking to me. There were no other beings in the lab at the time of the auditory stimulation. The voice described sensations of floating in liquid, lying on a cold, hard surface, and being touched on its side by the probe, all of which corresponded with the events that were occurring to the tissue. The embryo does not possess the cognitive or physical development necessary to produce audible, intelligent speech. I therefore deduced that the voice came from the soul of the embryo I was preparing to destroy. I came immediately to You to report my findings."

"We are willing to discuss what you have said, 2311-078-8489." With that, The Powerful Ones walked out of the room and left me sitting on the stone bench. I did not watch the moments pass on the time dial. I thought only of the embryo in the tiny glass tank.

After many moments had passed, They returned. In one collective voice They said, "It is Our decision that your report is invalid, based entirely on an unsubstantiated occurrence of soul speak. We have discussed the issue at length with the government from which we procured the embryos and have been assured that our procedures are legal by their laws. We have weighed the options and find that the good of the many, in this case the survival of the Adian race, must take precedence. You will return to Biolab immediately and proceed with the harvesting."

"But what about our law? If it has a soul, we are forbidden to harm it." I knew I risked punishment for articulating against Them, but I also knew I could not carry out Their decree. Either way, I would experience severe consequences.

"We are willing to discuss our law. If changes will need to be made, we will do so." They turned and left without further articulation.

I went back to Biolab. By now, it was late-of-day. The Twin Stars of Istman were fading with the setting sun. I was staring into the tank when I heard the voice again. "Tulin, I'm glad you're here."

I did not respond. Instead, I turned my visual sensors away from the pink mass.

"What's wrong, my friend? You are very sad."

I still did not answer immediately. Finally, I said, "First-of-day, when I placed you back in the tank, you asked me if I was The Creator."

"I remember. You never answered me."

"There is some information you do not know, information I was unable to articulate before. You are to be killed, and I am the one who is supposed to carry out the procedure."

This time the voice was silent. When it spoke again my auditory sensors detected a tremor in the tonality. "Is there nothing you can do to save me?"

"No, nothing. I will not take your life, but I cannot prevent it from being done."

"If I must die, I would ask two things of you, my friend. First, will you give me a name?"

I thought, but only for a moment. "There is a stream that flows through my village. It is pure and peaceful. I have spent some of the best moments of my existence on its banks. Its name is Avonya."

"Avonya," the voice said. "I like it. I like it a lot. Avonya it is. My second request will not be so easy. I want you to take my life."

"I cannot. I will not harm you."

"Don't you see, Tulin? My fate is sealed. You said so yourself. I want to die at the hands of someone who cares about me, someone who knows me, someone who will be gentle and kind. You have to do it. You are my only friend in this world."

I knew Avonya was right. I knew I could not trust this task to anyone else. I lifted the embryo from the chemical bath, positioned it under a microscope, and picked up the probe.

"Goodbye, Avonya," I said, as I turned on the suction. The machine and I both began to hum.

OVER TIME

Jeannine Baumgartle

I am nearly done
with evolving.
You'd think,
as early a start
as I got on it,
more would have happened.
The logical progression
from a single cell
to an "all you can be"
didn't happen.
There were stages,
adjustment periods,
rock/paper/scissors events.
Other selves to consider,
places to explore–
some more congenial
than others.
In this room
of quiet options,
I review the flowers
in the glass vase,
trace the stems
to where the water
is growing murky.

RED

Joy Kirchgessner

The AgriCeut Corporation freighter was on the last leg of its trip to a small planet they'd discovered six months prior. AgriCeut's procedure was to find new agricultural and drug resources by sending scout research teams into unknown territories. For three months now, harvesting equipment had operated on the surface transporting their cargo to orbiting freighters for processing. The end product was then shipped out to market.

Dr. Casey Post sat on her bed in her cramped living quarters peering out of her single port window and marveled at the inky blackness of space. This was her first off-world trip and everything was a source of wonder. Up until this point, she had worked at an AgriCeut-owned hospital on her home planet. Though the hospital environment was steeped in the day-to-day drama of health and sickness, she was surrounded by friends and co-workers with the same goal of saving lives. On board this ship, Casey found a mixture of occupations and purposes, most of which she had yet to learn.

She got up, showered in the small stall, pulled on her scrubs, clipped her communicator to her pants and tied back her hair. She thought she'd have an early meal in the mess hall, then return to the medical facilities and continue to orientate herself to her surroundings. She left her room for the empty tunnel-like hallway.

The freighter was a cavernous gray barge. Corridors branched out in every direction, leading to different sections. Even in her soft shoes, her footfalls made a metallic clank. She glanced at the arching metal ribs overhead, surreptitiously scanning for signs of structure fatigue. *Like I would recognize it if I saw it,* she thought. Everything had a utilitarian sparseness about it. This was a no-frills working ship. She wasn't sure how a three month stint inside this hunk of metal would affect her. She hoped she'd be too busy to think about it.

The smell of food reached her before she entered the mess hall. As she walked in she noticed a lot of other early risers—all of them male—watching her from benches and tables bolted to the floor. She cautiously crossed the room, making only slight eye contact and gave an uncertain nod of hello.

When she reached the food area, a rough-looking crew member approached. "Well, hello there. Just so happens I've got a table reserved for you and me."

"No, I don't think so," Casey said as she moved away from him and continued along the cafeteria line.

The man blocked her path and snarled, "Too good for me?"

"Let me pass."

He took hold of her elbow.

"Let go of me," she growled.

A commanding voice erupted from behind her, "You heard the Doc. Let go of her. You wouldn't want the *Doc* here to get the wrong impression. Think about it. You laying prone on a table in front of her one day and her standing over you with a knife."

The man grinned, then laughed. So did most of the crew in the mess. "You got a point, Captain." Releasing Casey's arm, he walked away.

Casey breathed a sigh of relief and turned, "Captain, is it?"

"That's what they tell me. Captain Nick Hudson." He smiled. "You'll have to forgive some of the crew members. Decorum is not a strong point out here. Would you care to sit at my table?"

"Thank you, Captain. Sure, I'd like that." They took seats at the rear of the mess.

Stirring sugar into his coffee, he asked, "How are the accommodations?"

"It's my maiden voyage into space and I'm finding it a little snug and dreary. And I can't say that I've ever been accosted in a lunch line before."

He chuckled. "I'm really a little surprised at AgriCeut sending a young doctor on this trip."

"Do you mean a young, inexperienced doctor or a young inexperienced female doctor?" She raised her eyebrow in a silent challenge.

He smiled. "That, too. You can see that most of the crew are male. And the nurses and doctors, well, they usually come a little more advanced in years."

"I owe AgriCeut three years for financing my education," she explained. "I volunteered for this project. Seemed intriguing. I've always been a great admirer of theirs. They've donated a lot of funds, not only for medical professionals and hospitals, but for many humanitarian purposes." She took a tentative sip of hot coffee. "What's your story?"

He looked down at his plate and scooped up a small bite of food with his fork. "Ten years with them."

Casey nodded, a little confused. "Tell me, Captain . . . What exactly are we doing on this trip?"

"Harvesting a red flower. There's acres of them down there on the surface. My job is to get them on this freighter and processed into a powder. What they're using the powder for, I haven't the slightest."

"Knowing AgriCeut, I'm sure it's something very beneficial." She could see she wasn't going to get much more out of him. "I really need to get back to the medical facilities," she said, as she got up from the bench. "There's so much I need to get organized. Thanks for your hospitality."

"It's been a pleasure. Let me know if there's anything I can do for you. We should be in orbit in a couple of days."

"Actually, there is one small thing, Captain. If the opportunity ever arises, I'd like to see the planet surface."

He nodded, "If the opportunity ever arises, I'll let you know."

Little occurred in the first couple of weeks other than minor injuries. She suspected drug use of a crew member named Pauley, who complained of aches requiring pain medications, with which he appeared much too familiar. She'd no doubt he had pain, but not of the kind that could be cured by more drugs.

He was sitting, hands on his knees, slightly bent forward on a chair in her office. They were having light conversation about his duties on the planet surface.

"What's the surface like?" Casey inquired, as she took a look at the inside of his ear with a scope while a male nurse stood in as assistant.

Pauley grinned with pleasure at the question. "You just wouldn't believe it. It's covered in red flowers. You'd think it was out of a fairy tale. When we run the harvesters through it, there's clouds of some kind of bug or more like butterflies pour out. Then just as sudden, they evaporate into the air. Just disappear."

"I'd love to see." She reached for a syringe from a tray. "Hold out your arm, I'm going to need a sample of your blood for the lab."

He anxiously rubbed his hand through his hair and got up. He fingered his communicator and it made a buzzing noise. "Love to, Doc. But gotta go—being paged. I'll be back to donate that blood." He spoke as he headed toward the door.

The nurse stepped in front of the exit and tried to stop him. "Don't think so, buddy. We need that sample."

Pauley looked at the nurse and then back at Casey.

"Let him leave. You'll be back, won't you, Pauley?" She was half surprised, half aggravated at the attendant.

"Sure thing, Doc," Pauley answered, brushing past the nurse.

"He needs to be reported to Security. That's the procedure," the nurse said with an air of authority.

"Need I remind you that this is my department, and I call the shots?" Casey said in an attempt to put him in his place. This wasn't the first time she'd run into this trouble.

Her attending medical personnel had been on several expeditions, of which they didn't share a lot in detail. Conversation was usually friendly, but when it came to the subject of what the Corporation was doing out here, the topic changed. They explained that they were all well paid and satisfied to just do their jobs. They suggested that she do the same.

About four weeks in, the Captain summoned her to go to the planet surface. He told her that the shuttle they were taking had a fully equipped medical bay and she didn't need to bring anything. Three of her companions were from research; she shook hands as they introduced themselves. Though the introduction was amicable, tension showed around their eyes.

"Remember you said 'if the opportunity arose'?" the Captain reminded her as he waved her to a seat behind his.

"I have a feeling this isn't a pleasure trip," she said, as she buckled in. Good or bad, she was happy to get off the ship for awhile.

"A native inhabitant was found near the harvest area. He's in bad shape. Thought you might be able to take a look at him and tell us what's going on," he explained as they pierced the atmosphere, sloping downward.

"A native? I thought . . . I guess I assumed . . . the planet was uninhabited."

"Information that there were some scattered tribes was on a need to know basis. And now . . . you need to know."

Casey glanced over at the researchers, who spoke quietly among themselves, inaudible to her ears. She had a growing sense of unease.

She turned her gaze to the window. The surface came more into focus. "And what do we know about these inhabitants, Captain?"

The question went unanswered as vegetation-covered hills fell away and a crimson valley spread out beneath them. Shafts of sunlight illuminated a meandering stream which formed a glistening boundary to an imposing mountain range. She was spellbound as the shuttle followed the valley to unending fields of red that rippled in an invisible breeze, and finally to the location where the combines were harvesting, leaving behind a dull brown path as they went. And just as Pauley had described, the most beautiful wave of shimmering insect wings poured out and just as quickly disappeared into the air.

The Captain landed the shuttle at the fringe of a brown field near the jungle-like foliage skirting the edges. They donned protective suits, gloves, and hoods safeguarding them from contaminants. Casey grabbed a medical case. Pauley met up with her and they proceeded cautiously to other crew members waiting at an area where on the ground, stones covered in red powder formed the outline of a sphere, the inside burned black. The body lay on its stomach, its head turned to the side. She knelt down beside the corpse, as the others circled around. The native's unburned skin was tattooed with what she assumed were red images of the insect and the flower they were harvesting.

Casey put a vital signs device on the body and took measurements. "He's dead," Casey said solemnly. "It appears he's hemorrhaged. I can't really tell you much more unless we can take him to the shuttle." She looked up at the Captain. Casey arose and stepped back to give the others room to move in.

"Pauley! Get a stretcher over here and get this body to quarantine!" Captain Nick barked the order.

Casey asked, "What's the meaning of the tattoos and the sphere?"

The Captain replied, "Looks like some sort of ritual."

"*Looks like*? Don't you know? Weren't there some sort of negotiations for this harvest?"

"It was assessed that there were just a few scattered primitive tribes. What's to negotiate?"

A crew member who'd gone with Pauley to get a stretcher came running and screamed, "Hurry —Pauley's sick! I left him in the shuttle bay." Reaction was swift. Casey and the others followed the nearly hysterical crewman back to the shuttle.

Pauley lay on an examining table, bleeding from his nose and ears. "Hey Doc, I hurt," he rasped. "I really *do* this time. I'm so *cold*." He shivered, intermittently coughing up a little blood. "I only took a little of it. Do you think that's what made me sick?"

Casey put on a mask and rubber gloves then bent over him concerned. "Took a little of what, Pauley? What did you take?"

"The red powder. It was supposed to be the best. I thought I'd try it."

"The powder we're processing here?"

Something wriggled in the oozing blood from his nose, twisting back and forth. *Some sort of larvae*, she thought. Confused and repulsed, she turned to the researchers standing near and asked them to take a look.

One of them took a fluid sample and carefully placed it under a microscope.

With urgency in his voice, he told the Captain, "Something's gone wrong. The powder's contaminated. We've got to get rid of it."

Casey, intent and adamant, demanded, " Got to get rid of it?

Wait a minute... *Someone* is going to tell me what's going on here." She took a resentful step toward the Captain. "This has something to do with the flower, doesn't it?"

"Poor Pauley. Just had to steal a little of the red stuff. Good for us, bad for him." He looked Casey in the eye and said, "Get out of my face, Doc."

She didn't budge. "Not until you tell me what I need to know."

He spoke through his communicator to the orbiting freighters. "Security—the powder's contaminated. Discharge the loads into space. Contact headquarters. Get the harvesters off the planet."

"Say what Captain?" came the crewman's response.

The Captain shouted into the communicator, "Didn't you hear me? I said *move!*"

He stared at Casey and bristled. "It's a *drug*, Doc. They thought a very lucrative hallucinogen. Sends you on a high like no other ever before. Research said there were no side effects. They've been testing that stuff for months. I can only guess the current season and the insects have something to do with the change."

"And...just what do you intend to do about it?" She spat out the words.

"I'm doing it, Doc."

"What about the people who bought this powder? The planets it went to? How do we know other loads weren't contaminated? How do we know that this insect isn't using us to spread to other planets? As soon as I get off this vessel I can do something about it. I'll go to the authorities. *Everyone* will know about AgriCeut's secret business."

He smiled wryly. "And kill all that *humanitarian* effort? Destroy your career and get nowhere? No you won't, Doc. Best you can do is help minimize the damage. It'll be taken off the market. You don't think they sold it under any name that could be traced back to them do you?" He paused, as comprehension came over his face. "You really *are* naively altruistic. Something vaguely attractive about that." He put his hand on her shoulder. "Relax, you're one of us now. Gets more intriguing all the time, doesn't it?" He turned his back and walked away, still handing out orders.

Anger flooded over her as she realized the situation AgriCeut had put her in. She thought, *Yes, I'll go along with it. Until I get back home. Then they'll see how I 'minimize the damage'.*

INFINITY, ETERNITY

Marian Allen

Eternity is not everlasting
it is
now
always
now

Infinity is not vast
it is
here
here
       unbounded

Infinity
       Eternity
Are interminably
small

Infinity, Eternity previously appeared in the **Serendipity Sampler**.

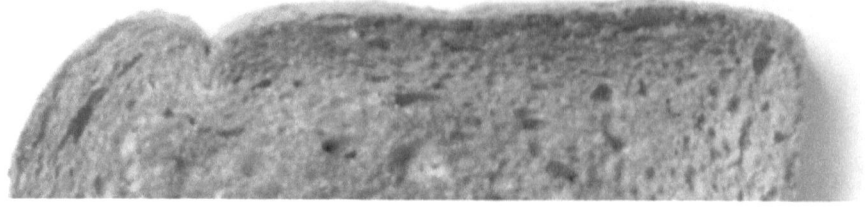

QUANTUM TOAST
Ginny Fleming

It all started with my morning toast.

Breakfast. The most important meal of the day. That day, *my* breakfast changed time. It *freakin' changed time.* Looking back, I now wonder: What if, instead of a simple breakfast of toast, grape jam and juice, I'd chosen *that* day to waste my morning nutrition on a fat-filled serving of Mickey-D's? I wonder, and I *will* wonder about this for the rest of my days . . . .

I'm a journalist. Not a vastly important one, but I like to think I found my niche in "serving mankind" journalism. I work for the Nationwide Enquirer. My beat covers nutcases. Needless to say, I've seen it all and then some. Everything from A— "Alien Mail-Order Bride" to Z— "Zombie-Bat-Boy". And *I'm* the guy the nutcases send *their* nutcase treasures to. I've got stuff here in my apartment that'll curl your hair... or make you bust a gut, however *you* view nutcase journalism. Why, just the other day, some crazy sent me a little jelly jar filled with what he called "alien plasma" that he claimed to have smuggled out of Area 51. Said he didn't know the shelf life, but the little alien he claimed to have befriended—Bloop, I think his name was—said it could send the Space Shuttle on a five year mission or make your Pacer shut down a Hemi. Your choice. Told me it was some powerful shit that the government claimed didn't exist. Then he added: "Bloop said take care not to get any on your clothes or hands—but if you do—under all circumstances, *don't suck your fingers.* Oh . . . and be sure to refrigerate it after opening." Yeah, right.

I thought about filing it under "Things My Momma Told Me To Ignore"—drop it in my circular file, so to speak—but at the last minute I stored it in my fridge. Next to my fruity jellies and jams. Can you say BIG mistake, boys and girls? . . . I knew you could. Sigh.

Anyhow, the morning I've since come to think of as "The Dawning of the Quantum Toast" really began the night before. Mindy, my girlfriend of two years, informed me she was moving on, regretting the time she'd spent with a man like me—a hard-case shit-cake (her words). She said: "You never cared about anything or anyone but yourself. If a little old lady fell at your feet, you'd use her for a footpath to keep your Nikes dry." She said: "The whole country's rethinking lifestyles, concentrating on only the important things, only the things truly needed—downsizing, as it were—and I'm following America's lead. I'm downsizing *you*. In my life, you're just not needed—in fact, you're no longer *in* my life. You're a debit and not an asset, and I'm getting my accounts in order." To put it simply, she said: *I was toast*.

Looking at my breakfast and thinking back on her words the night before, I snickered. I sobbed. Then I laughed again and spoke aloud to the room, startling Blinky, my cat. "Toast. The lady said I was *toast*. Said 'you ain't never cared bout nutten or no one else but yur'own damn self.'"

Mindy. She might not have great command of the Queen's English, but my Mindy's a good judge of character. I spread a generous dollop of grape jam on my still-warm toast, took a bite and my "world" blipped. Blipped for the merest fraction of a moment.

I gripped the table and closed my eyes against a sudden vertigo. When I opened them, things . . . *many things*, had changed. Oh, I was still eating my breakfast. I just wasn't in *my* apartment, eating my breakfast. From all appearances, this *was* my apartment, but it wasn't. Little things were vastly different. Like my kitchen.

My kitchen: The configuration was basically the same, but certain items were missing. Coffeemaker, microwave, digital clock—gone. All the remaining appliances were... *different*. Instead of the fancy Jenn-Aire range, a small white gas range stood in its place. Instead of an LCD-TV on the wall, an old-fashioned radio sat under a crude painting of the Alps. And my new huge ice dispenser refrigerator had been replaced by a small box with a Robby the Robot "head-thingy" on top. The wheeze from the antique caused me to think it was even older than I first thought.

"Oh, Lord," I whispered. "What's going on here?" My fearful eyes searched for Blinky. Me and that cat had been together for five long years. Thankfully, a moment's search found him sunning himself in a patch of shine pouring through the window.

It was on very shaky legs I staggered over, toast still in hand. Raising the window, I gazed out at the view from my Wichita third floor apartment. Outside, a massive political rally goose-stepped up the boulevard. *Goose-stepped???* WTF? I looked closer . . . .

Sure enough, the goose-stepping soldiers carried red flags bearing swastikas, and I quickly figured out this was *not* the street where I parked my car.

I almost took another bite of "Bloopy-Toast", then, thought better of it and dropped it out the window where a yappy dog ran up, ate it, and promptly "blipped" out of sight. "Blinky?" I murmured, "We're *definitely* not in Kansas anymore . . . ."

The first thing I did was store the Bloopy-Jam at the back of the wheezy fridge. Then, after a frantic search of my "new" apartment, I found an identity card. Heh. Don't know why I called it an *identity card*. It was just some German words and a name on white cardboard. It declared me to be an honored member of Hitler's SS.

It took me three days to gather the courage to leave my apartment. Good thing I had plenty of toast—the safe kind—or I'd've starved to death. As we couldn't find any Meow Mix, Blinky almost didn't fare as well. But in the end, he settled for canned salmon.

Two years later, I'd managed to use some fairly weak high school German combined with some phenomenally good college history and I'd risen in the ranks of Hitler's SS. I'll not reveal my pseudo-Nazi name—but just know when you read your history books, my name *is* there. In fact, I was one of der Führer's fav-boys. Now, please don't get me wrong. I *wasn't* a "loyal numbnut Nazi". In fact, every time I had to crow: "Heil", I very nearly lost my lunch. But, I figured, *if* I was stuck in Hitler's Germany, I should at least make myself useful.

I intended to kill Adolf Hitler.

Aw, go on. Admit it. Haven't we *ALL* wanted to go back in time and do the man? Lucky me. I had the chance.

To shorten the telling, I'll just say I made numerous attempts. All failures. All merely made the monster appear clumsy. I came to think perhaps Hitler could only die on the actual reported death date. He would die when he would die—but I'd be damned if I wasn't the man for the job. Call it personal satisfaction, if you will. So, I bided my time and tried not to think of the innocent masses he killed every day. Mindy would've been so proud of me. I finally cared about someone other than myself—and it ripped my heart out daily . . . .

Then the calender told me we were approaching "D-Day" for Hitler. Der Führer took up residence in the Führerbunker on the 16th of January, 1945. Gossip said he was already crazier than a shithouse rat, and as one of his personal assistants, I adamantly believed it.

Blinky and I spent a hellish three months and a nickel in what became der Führer's Love-Shack, and I tried my best to keep my feline friend confined to my matchbox-size quarters, because of the "Big Boss Man's" reported hatred of cats. When I could, Blinky was tethered. Oh, how he loved that . . . .

Day by day, Hitler grew stranger (Ha! That's like saying Jack the Ripper was a bad blind date), but from my standout college history grades, I knew our time in the bunker grew short. Some of us realized that his mind truly snapped after April 22nd. He started talking defeat. He rambled on about suicide. Don't know just how many of my bunker-mates realized how dire the situation was becoming, but a few of us were sweating bullets while averting our eyes from one another. This was sehr schlecht . . . bad. Very bad, indeed.

Then April 28th reared its ugly head. And on the night of Blondi's needless poisoning, I knew the end was hours away—whether by my hand or not. You see, Dr. Haase's pet's demise set the death-clock ticking. A paranoid Hitler believed the SS cyanide was bogus, and so instructed his physician to try it out on the hapless pooch. Blondi gave her life for the Third Reich, and I tightened my Blinky-Watch. In fact, I took to carrying Blinky everywhere I went.

After midnight on April 29th, Hitler married Eva Braun in a small civil ceremony in a map room within the bunker complex. She was a pretty little thing, and I liked her. She reminded me of a blonde Mindy. Afterward, Hitler hosted a modest wedding breakfast with his new wife, then took his secretary into another room and dictated his last will and testament. He signed these documents in the pre-dawn hours and then retired to bed. I almost felt pity for Eva . . . almost. She'd certainly made her bed and she'd die in it. You know what they say: Marry a murderous monster, wake up dead . . . or something like that.

I'd set a running countdown in my head. Adolf and Eva enjoyed the better part of two days in wedded, blissful insanity and I ticked off the remaining minutes. Some historians say Hitler died by his own hand in their bunkered honeymoon suite, after poisoning his new bride. Some say the killer-nutjob escaped to South America and lived out his last days sunning his scrawny ass on a sandy beach. And some say Hitler hitched a ride on the Mothership with Elvis and Amelia Earhart. Me? I was still determined that a certain time-challenged journalist would yet be the death of Hitler. So . . . I fixed der Führer und *seine errötende Braut* (his blushing bride) a last late night snack. Toast. I fixed him toast.

After knocking politely, I entered the bridal suite, pushing a serving cart upon which rested a lazy susan laden with streusel, juice, coffee, warm toast points and an assortment of jams. The time we'd spent in this hell of a cave, I'd done my homework. I found out grape jam was Mr. and Mrs. Hitler's least favorite flavor. So, I'd swirled the poison into the rest of the selections. The marmalade alone would've killed a cow. My hopeful escape plan, my Bloopy-Jam, was by my right hand and Blinky was hidden in a carrier under the serving cart's tablecover. I was loaded for bear.

"Heil, Hitler!" I saluted in that hateful manner. "Herr Führer, Meine Dame, perhaps an early breakfast would be to your liking? I have some lovely . . . *toast.*" I smiled ingratiatingly. Then I raised my eyes and noticed Eva slumped on the sofa next to the crazy man. Ohhh . . . I'd come too late for the blonde. He'd already slipped her the cyanide cocktail. "Ach, Herr Führer," I began, "was ist los?"

"My love . . . *Meine Liebe, Sie schläft.* She sleeps."

I was speechless. He sat there cradling her head as if he'd given her a great gift. It sickened me. But if I thought I'd seen it all, nothing prepared me for what he did next. Hitler rang a tiny bell and called another assistant's name. "Johann!" He sternly ordered, "Send in mein Doppelgänger! Schnell!"

. . . and in walked . . . *Hitler.*

It was uncanny, the resemblance between the two. Right down to the shiny gold buttons.

Hitler . . . the *real* Hitler, pulled a Luger from his holster and motioned the fake Führer closer. With a few words, the real deal forced his lookalike to take his place on the sofa and made him cradle the unfortunate Frau Hitler's limp body in his arms. Seconds later, a shot rang out and fake Hitler slumped dead, the Luger's concussion sending Eva's corpse to the other side of the couch.

He pointed the still warm Luger at me. "Und jetzt," the smiling Führer whispered, "es ist Ihre zeit." *And now, it's your time . . . .* I cursed my newly acquired second language.

"Mein Führer . . . ." I murmured, "might I have a last request?" I eyed the grapey Bloopy-Jam. "A last bite of toast?"

"Aber natürlich." *But of course,* my insane leader granted. I quickly spread the hopeful grapey savior across a toast point and raised it to my lips while I reached under the serving cart for my cat.

Then to my horror, Hitler grabbed the toast from my hand. "Dies scheint schmackhaft." He said it looked tasty to him, grinned, popped the Bloopy-covered treat in his mouth and just like that yappy dog from two years prior, Adolf "blipped" from my sight. The Luger dropped to the floor at the dead doppelgänger's feet.

I was flabbergasted. Scant moments passed, but Blinky came to my rescue rousing me outta my stupor with a plaintive and mournful "meow". I quickly gathered my furry child into my arms, spread another toast point with the purpley goo and sighed. "Guess Hitler's painting roses in Argentina . . . . and Blinky? You an' me . . . we're on the road again!" I bit the toast and found I was growing kinda fond of the sickly sweet taste. "There's no place like ho—"

BLIP

LONELY IS THE NIGHT

Dirk Griffin

earth alone
turning traveling
beside its single
moon knows
the darkness
miles beyond
the sun

and the moon
hidden from
our star's
warmth far
forgotten
from its
fiery stare

shadows slink
around the
blue
how lonely
is the night
eclipsed
i wait for
you

Lonely is the Night previously appeared at **www.everydaypoets.com**.

UNIVERSE TIME

Bonnie Abraham

Ziggy Malloy flipped her cell phone onto her bed, put her hands on her hips and glared in the mirror, as though *she* were the one who had just ended her plans to go to the beach for a few days. "Aren't I supposed to be on leave?" she demanded of the scowling face.

"Malloy. Report back to the compound before midnight." The call had been from her supervisor, Joe Noonan. He hadn't waited for arguments.

"Who does he think I am, his slave?" grumbled Ziggy. But she repacked her work gear and caught the next bus.

The two-hour trip to the Tomorrow Today Institute compound (dear old TTI to its employees) was filled with questions. Why had she been called back? Was she in some kind of trouble? Had she forgotten part of her duties before she left? Was some important project behind schedule? But the *big* question was, "Why me?"

Randy Phelps met her at the bus stop and drove her into the compound. "Noonan says to say he's sorry about your leave, but he thinks you'll forgive him when you see what's up."

"Just what *is* up?" she asked, figuring this for an opening.

"You'll have to wait," said Randy. He looked like he had just beaten someone to the last piece of candy.

"Come on, man. You know you wanna tell me."

Randy shook his head. "No way am I gonna risk makin' the man mad tonight."

That was a first. Randy was always in trouble

with Noonan. He lived for it. Ziggy tried a few more ploys, but Randy, for once, didn't budge. Maybe she slammed the car door a little hard when she got out. She figured he'd get over it.

She reported to Noonan's office before she went to her quarters. That's how curious she was. Her athletic shoes squeaked on the polished blue tiles in the hall, causing the few uniformed employees she encountered to turn heads in her direction, their eyes full of suspicion.

"Why aren't you in uniform?" was Noonan's first question when she entered his office unannounced. He hadn't even looked up.

"Wanted to see what this was about," she said, barely containing her irritation.

He looked up, then. "Sit, and don't interrupt."

She sat.

"You have been selected for a special top-secret team, as of this morning. One of the previous members of the team failed the physical. Because of the nature of the project you will be involved with, they are insisting that you take *your* physical before you are briefed. They don't want another person running around with top-secret information who isn't in the project. So I can't tell you what it's about. But I think, when you hear, you will want to be involved. You are to report to Medical as soon as you change into uniform."

Ziggy waited a minute to be sure he was finished. "*They* being?" She let her voice trail off. She had thought Noonan was the boss.

"*They* being the ones who are funding the project."

"And that would be?" But Noonan only shook his head. "What if I don't want to be on this team after I find out what it is?"

"You will. Trust me on this, Malloy. It's big."

"But if I don't?"

"Let's hope that doesn't happen." It sounded like a warning.

"Right. Medical."

When Ziggy had completed the physical—one that was so basic she wondered how anyone breathing could have failed it—she was given a pass, which she was instructed to wear at all times inside the restricted area. She was shown down a long narrow hall to a door, where she was abandoned by her guide with a cheery, "Good luck." The door read: RESTRICTED AREA in three-inch-high red block letters. She wondered if she should knock.

Breathe. You have a pass; just go in. She turned the handle and entered.

An oversized football-player type growled, "Pass?" then nodded as she showed him the plastic tag. "You the new one? Report to Dr. Edmond. Room 4. Down that hall on the right." He pointed and waited for her to move.

"Thanks." She tried not to let her knees buckle as she complied.

Dr. Edmond turned out to be a thin, leathery man with a fringe of white hair and eyes like blue agates. "Ah. Miss Malloy. Welcome to the team. I apologize for the short notice. I'm afraid it means you won't get much training, but I am given to understand that you already have most of the skills we require. I'm sure it won't be a problem."

He rose from his desk chair as she entered, coming to meet her and escort her to the sofa placed at an angle across one corner of the large room. "Would you like a coffee? Or tea, perhaps? I prefer tea but most of the team act as though coffee is an absolute necessity—so we have both." He smiled and poured himself a mug of tea as he talked.

"I'm a coffee junky," she said. "Black." She sat down on the edge of the sofa and found that even from the edge, its soft cushions drew her in. There was something unsettling about its coercive offer of comfort. She took the thick blue mug Dr. Edmond handed her and bit her tongue to keep from asking what this was all about. She'd known the man only a few seconds but already sensed that he was not someone to be hurried.

As though reading her thoughts, her host took the seat opposite her—a delicate French Louis-the-whatever-number affair—and said, "I'm sure you are wondering just what we do?" When she agreed, he continued, "We have been doing research in time travel." He waited a moment for her to digest this. "I know that most of the scientific community believe that such a thing is impossible. However, I can now say, it is not only possible, but we have done it." His enthusiasm pushed him from the chair and he paced to the door and back. "Well *I* have not—not yet. But part of our team has." He placed his mug of tea carefully on the stand and turned to her again. "Now I must ask. Are you in? Because if you are not—"

The silence hung between them like thick fog. Ziggy wasn't sure what to think. Time travel was theoretically impossible. She knew the data. It was one of her special interests. *So either this nice old gentleman is loony or all the data is wrong.* She felt like she was missing something. She took a deep breath. *Time travel!* "In," she said.

That was all two weeks ago. Time. What a nebulous thing it had become in those two weeks. The first week was spent with masses of data sheets, diagrams and mission reports. Ziggy learned the rudiments of *correct* time travel science and then the practical skills—what buttons did what and what *not* to wear when traveling to 16 AD.

The second week—well, that isn't quite correct but how does one quantify something as indeterminate as time—Ziggy *traveled*. She spent three months in the 1980 version of TTI, where she met a much younger version of Dr. Edmond. He had been just as eager and intense, and just as methodical. His superiors thought him not a little insane in his pursuits. Concepts like time travel were strictly for science fiction. The big test of the mission had been not to disclose to Dr. Edmond that he was correct.

When Ziggy returned to the present, she had been gone only a day. Each mission required a minimum one-day debriefing period; the first one was more a period of adjustment. After all, she had just lived three months that didn't exist.

Her second mission, two days later, was much trickier. She was to travel away from the institute once she arrived at her time-destination. She was not told beforehand when she would arrive, but Dr. Edmond assured her that her pass would take care of any problems—at least while she remained in the institute.

When she stepped out of the time device—which looked like a huge sandstone rock on the outside—she was met by a Dr. Edmond who looked much like the one she had just left. Excitedly, he gave her an envelope, a purse and a coat. "It's cold," he explained. "The envelope has your instructions and the purse has identification, money and tickets. Good luck." He walked her to the door of the embarkation room and opened it, waving her through.

Once she was in the hall, the door closed behind her with a soft click. She was alone. Fingers shaking, she tore into the envelope and found that she was to report to her old high school where she was to spend the day as a substitute science teacher. Her instructions suggested she disguise herself with a wig, and perhaps some make-up. "You will find the technicians in room 72B ready to assist you," said the letter. She reported to 72B.

An hour later, Ziggy emerged from 72B, looking like she was at least 50, with close-cropped greying hair and horn-rimmed glasses. She was dressed in a drab grey suit and black oxfords—shoes her mother used to call *sensible*. She checked the digital watch she had been given by one of the technicians. He had told her it was set to military time. It read 5:14. She was to report to her old school at 7:45.

She made her way out of the Institute, getting curious glances but no challenges. She caught the bus to her hometown and then nervously reexamined her mission. She had not been told that she was about to meet herself, but the clues were obvious. She tried to remember a day in her past when she had had a substitute science teacher named Ann Martin. Was she creating a new past for herself, or did she need to do this mission because it had already happened in some cyclical universe? Or was this an experiment to see what would happen? Was she about to change her own past by her influence on an impressionable high school student? Her instructions did not say what she was to accomplish.

By the time Ziggy reported to the principal's office, she had conjectured all manner of terrible consequences. To her dismay, her hand shook when she presented her ID to the secretary.

"Oh, yes. Miss Martin," said the plump, friendly woman. Ziggy recognized her face, but couldn't remember her name. "Here is your schedule. All your classes are in the same room. That should make it easier for you." She called out to a slender girl with long, straight brown hair who was passing the door. "Karen, would you please show Miss Martin where the science room is?"

As the girl waited, slouching against the doorframe, the secretary gave Ziggy a handbook of rules and a floor plan of the school. "You *should* find the lesson plans on the desk." Her tone said she probably wouldn't. "Let me know if you need anything."

Ziggy thanked her and followed Karen down the hall to the science room. She recognized the girl as one of the popular ones in the class after her own. She had *not* been popular with the teachers. Ziggy wondered if Karen had a science class this term.

The room was exactly as Ziggy remembered it, half lab and half classroom. It smelled faintly of sulfur and chalk dust. A row of equations lined the chalkboard. A dented and chipped metal desk was shoved back in one corner. There was a manila folder in the center of the otherwise bare desk. She breathed a sigh of relief. Lesson plans.

The day progressed uneventfully through the first six periods. It was the seventh that she was worried about. That's when the seniors had science. *She* was a senior. Or, at least one of her was. She had looked over the lesson. It was cell theory, nothing about time or time travel. Of course, by *her* time, cell theory had been drastically advanced. Theory only being hinted at had become proven fact. She wondered again at her purpose.

Class began with a pop quiz. There were only twelve students and they all passed the quiz. They discussed the questions the students missed and then moved on to the reading assignment. Ziggy was surprised at their understanding of the material. In her memory of high school, the students went to class only half prepared at best. She guessed they had been better than she remembered. *She*—the other Ziggy—didn't volunteer much in class, but knew the answers when called on.

They ran out of planned material a few minutes before class was to be over. "Anyone have other questions?" Ziggy asked. Then instantly wished she could take back the words. Asking a class of high-school seniors such an open question was inviting trouble.

Young Ziggy raised her hand.

"Ziggy, isn't it?" asked the Miss Martin Ziggy, knowing full well, it was.

"Yes. Do *you* believe we will ever be able to travel in time?"

Ziggy gulped. She carefully pushed the annoying horn-rimmed glasses back in place to give herself time to think. "The current science is not hopeful," she said, trying to remember what the current science *was*. "However, I believe the same thing was once said about flying."

The class laughed and then, thankfully, the bell rang. The room cleared, as though someone had yelled, "Fire!" Ziggy made a few notes for the regular teacher regarding how things had gone and thanked him for the excellent lesson plans, then collected her purse and returned, per instructions, to TTI.

The compound was on night shift. The guard at the gate waved her through when she flashed her pass. The embarkation room was empty. She entered the time capsule, set it to return her to one hour after departure, strapped in, and smiled as she pressed the large green button marked "GO". She wondered, as she had the first time, just whose idea *that* had been.

Dr. Edmond was waiting for her. As was Randy Phelps.

"Randy?" she said as she exited the chamber. "What are you doing here?"

"Randy is one of our travelers, now," explained Dr. Edmond. "Did you enjoy your little teaching excursion?"

"It was a little scary," Ziggy admitted, "but I think it went okay."

Dr. Edmond nodded. "No anomalies have been detected. Now, let's all have some tea—or coffee—and chat."

Two days of chats (Dr. Edmond's term for the debriefing meetings) and sleep followed. To Ziggy's surprise, Randy was included in several of the chats. She asked Dr. Edmond about why she had been sent back to meet herself. She now found that she vaguely remembered a conversation with a substitute teacher about time travel, but she had not been able to remember it when she was on her way to the school as Miss Martin.

Dr. Edmond shrugged. "We found in your records that a Miss Martin had substituted one day in your science class during your senior year, and it appears that it was at that same time that you really became interested in time travel—checking out books in the library on the subject and so forth. But we could find no Miss Martin in other records." His blue eyes danced with light. "It is a pleasing puzzle, isn't it?"

Ziggy shivered. Dr. Edmond wasn't telling her *everything*. She didn't know *how* she knew that, but she knew.

On the third day after the school mission, Dr. Edmond announced the next one. "It will be a two-person task. We've done that before, but only for short hops. This one will be longer." He paused to take a slow sip of tea, his eyes shining above the mug. "*Much* longer."

Ziggy hadn't really been paying attention to his words and was startled at Randy's intense, "*How* long?"

"About 10,000 years," came the soft reply.

She almost dropped her mug.

"End of the Ice Age—mastodons," murmured Randy.

Dr. Edmond bounced out of his chair and paced, waiving his mug of tea dangerously. "Just imagine! You will be able to *document* what we have only been able to interpret from the fossils!"

As Randy and Dr. Edmond discussed what they expected to find, Ziggy kept silent, wondering. She had studied the old earth/new earth debate and wasn't at all convinced by the data assembled by the old earth proponents. She sank back into the coercive comfort of the sofa and smiled. They were about to settle the argument.

It was two weeks before all the preparations could be made for the Benchmark Mission, as it had been named by some unknown power. Ziggy and Randy studied the plethora of material, attempting to create strategies for all the various contingencies. The task was mind-boggling.

At last the day arrived. Ziggy and Randy, dressed ridiculously in artificial fur, stepped into the time capsule—which had been raised several feet from its previous location to account for erosion—and closed the door. Alone with him, in the silent chamber, Ziggy felt suddenly awkward.

"Well, here we are," he said.

"Yes. Here we are."

Randy sat down at his station and strapped himself in. Ziggy took a deep breath and followed his example.

"You want to do the honors?" he asked, pointing at the panel.

Their destination was already programmed in. All that was left to do was to press the button. "Have you ever wondered whose idea it was to write 'GO' on it?" she asked.

Randy laughed. "Yes. It reminds me of a comic book."

"A *very old* comic book," she agreed. She took another deep breath and pushed the big green button.

Ziggy woke first. That turned out to be a good thing. On previous trips she had experienced only a slight sensation of falling, like one feels as an elevator begins to descend, or like the stomach lurch at the top of a long roller coaster drop. They had been warned to expect a *more severe experience*. They had not been told they would probably pass out. Nor were they actually *told* they might become nauseous. So waking first saved her the embarrassment of losing her lunch in front of Randy, who would have made the most of the opportunity to humiliate her for the rest of her life. Thankfully, too, she had been briefed on the whereabouts of the waste receptacles so there was no mess to clean up.

She had returned to her seat and was checking their location and status when Randy woke with a groan—and then a curse as he plummeted out of his chair to the waste bin. She vowed to be kind. After all, she could afford to be. She now had the advantage.

It was then she realized, she still wasn't feeling so well, herself. The capsule seemed to be moving. No, she analyzed. That wasn't the right word. Floating. That was the sensation. She pushed a few buttons, opening various view screens. Blackness.

"We seem to have arrived at night," said Ziggy.

Randy was back in his chair, holding his head with both hands, his elbows anchored on his knees. "That's good. No observers of our arrival."

She agreed, but something just didn't feel right. "It's *really* dark out there," she said.

Randy raised his head and peered at the view screen in front of him. He frowned. "Where are the stars?" He looked around at the other screens. "No stars! And where's the moon?" He punched buttons on the console, refreshing the screens, checking the settings. "Something's not right, Ziggy."

She grimaced. Randy's observation backed up her own feelings. "Do you still feel like we're floating?"

"Yeh. I wonder how long that will last?"

The feeling didn't go away. They waited for daylight, but it didn't arrive. They had been watching monitors and napping from boredom for about eight hours when they noticed that the cabin felt stuffy. Randy checked the air quality monitor.

"The oxygen level is dropping. We need to open the circulation vents," he said, his fingers already on the keys.

"Wait!" yelled Ziggy. Then more calmly, she added, "Let's check the outside atmosphere first—just to be safe." She tapped in the codes and got—H_2O. "We're under water?"

Randy was suddenly peering over her shoulder at the screen. "What the . . . ?"

Words from the Bible popped into her head. "And the Spirit of God moved upon the face of the waters. And God said, 'Let there be light,'" she quoted.

As though her own words had brought it about, there was a sudden frying sound. Every view screen flared with eye piercing light. Ziggy shielded her eyes and tried to see something in the brightness, but it was impossible. The air was getting hot.

"Set the return coordinates!" she screamed.

Randy was still trying to see something on the view screens. "What's going on?" he demanded. The walls began to glow red.

She pushed him aside and entered coordinates, hoping she was doing it correctly. She didn't take time to double-check what she had entered; she slammed her hand on "GO" and fell to the floor. Everything went black again.

Ziggy sat in a lounge chair, her legs covered by a powder-blue, knitted afghan. She stared across the small pond at the muted reds and oranges of the trees on the other side. The air crackled with frost not yet burned away by the sun. A brief gust blew a strand of her grey hair across her wrinkled cheek and she pushed it away as the sound of footsteps caused her to turn. "Ah. Dr. Edmond."

The young man bent to hand her a steaming mug. "Black? No sugar? Did I get it right?"

She smiled briefly, deepening the lines around her eyes. "Yes, exactly. Thank you. Has there been word from the hospital yet?"

Dr. Edmond lowered his bright blue eyes. "He made it through the operation, but he's still critical. The surgeon believes there's a good chance he won't have any permanent brain damage but his burns are severe."

"Poor Randy. He took the brunt of it. If only I had realized sooner."

Dr. Edmond sat down on the damp grass, facing her. "Miss Malloy, I wish you would tell me what happened—where you came from."

For a moment, Ziggy was silent as she considered the things

she had learned—and the awful cost. She examined the blue veins of the hand that held the shaky mug. Time travel aged. One would think I would have become younger, she mused to herself. Still, she could prove nothing. The ship was destroyed. Randy might or might not survive. There was only her word. She tightened her grip, steadying the cup and made her decision.

Ziggy shook her head. "I think that would not be wise, just yet." But someday, she thought, *someday* I will get the proof.

"The few instruments we have recovered from that machine you arrived in seem to be from some sort of time travel device—much more advanced than anything I have been able to come up with. Will you at least verify that you are from the future?" When she didn't answer, he pressed on. "The fur clothing you wore was fake, very convincing—more convincing than any I've seen before, but still fake. That and the advanced instruments we were able to salvage indicate you were from the future planning to travel to the past. Did you *miss* your destination?"

"Ah, a *pleasing puzzle* for you?" There was the slightest hint of sarcasm in her voice. "Where am I—or rather, when am I from? When was I meant to go—to go *to*? Oh—it's so hard to express. And I can't answer. I'm not sure, myself. Not pleasing to *me*, my good doctor."

"But you *have* traveled in time?" insisted the doctor. "It does work?"

"Is time travel possible?" She leaned back in her chair. "I asked *myself* that once. And I—very wisely, I think—answered that current science is not hopeful. But science also once said that about flying, I believe." She took a sip of her coffee and shrugged. "Who knows what the future holds. We don't even know the past, yet." But I *will* find out, she added to herself.

GREENSLEEVES

Jeannine Baumgartle

When we started thinking
of planets as having genders,
our frame of reference
shifted toward relationship
with them and with each other.
A renaissance, we called it.
Reality shifted so quickly,
that information could
no longer be understood
even in technical terms
except through metaphor.
Art and music flourished
as we struggled to refine
our identity among worlds
and to preserve a future.
In a way, we went backwards.
Whole cities emptied into
sustainable communities
for whom daily commerce
was in walking distance.
Energy consumption dwindled;
people with a context
managed themselves,
learned to be creative.
Equations had lyrics.
For love of life
we sang Greensleeves.

REBEL

Samantha Lopez

On her way back to the residence towers, Morgan closed her eyes against the pain in her head. The hum of the helicopters increased the throbbing, but, though she'd never admit it, the copter's thrum also gave her a feeling of comfort. She knew her mother was probably on one of the craft. Morgan's mother spent as much time exploring as she did sending criticizing e-mails, probably more. Still, it was nice feeling a little closer to her mother, if only physically. Located on her mother's work-site base, Langburg Academy's uniquely designed iridescent dome arched high overhead, keeping native flora and fauna safely outside. The Academy—contained under the dome—was terraformed, complete with Earth grass, leafy trees and cement sidewalks.

Outside the "bubble of normal", dead trees composed the native terrain, though, due to the air quality, scientists knew photosynthesis occurred somewhere. Her biologist mother worked to solve that very mystery, and to explore the possibilities of expanding the habitable part of the planet. Once they accomplished that task, perhaps she'd actually get to see her mother now and then.

The sunlight coming through the shielded eco-bubble transmuted into a soft purplish hue, thanks to the iridescence of the dome. She squinted against the sunlight reflecting off the incoming helicopter as a sharp arc of pain shot through her head. *Another migraine.* The headaches had begun a few weeks earlier and were becoming more frequent. Today's was bad enough the nurses had sent her back to her dorm to rest.

The ground seemed to shift beneath her. Tightening her grasp on her backpack, Morgan realized she'd been the one to move, not the ground. She fought the urge to crawl on her hands and knees back to her dorm room. That way, at least the ground would stay still.

This is ridiculous.

Deciding to take the path to the furthest door from the airport, she felt the vertigo increase, but the headache lessen. The sudden sensation of being above her surroundings caused her to grimace.

Great, I'm going insane as well as being in pain.

Straying off the normal path, she cut across the grass. A decorative stone bench placed near a set of Earth trees overlooked a reflecting pool. She took a seat. The mild vertigo was still with her when a small mew sounded overhead.

In the closest tree, a large kitten or small cat, about a foot in length, gripped a low branch. Its soft, gray fur was decorated with black stripes on its face, legs and tail, and black spots on its body. It mewed plaintively.

A cat? There were no free-roaming animals allowed in the compound. The creature must have escaped from the lab just up the path.

"I should return you," she informed the cat. She set down her backpack and climbed on the bench to reach the branch. The cat sniffed curiously at her hand. She gently picked up the creature and held it close to her chest, and climbed down off the bench.

She knew animals were the first to be exposed to the foreign planet's environment to try to gauge what might happen to a human. Her mother had told her about the rats. She wasn't as torn by rats. The kitten purred contentedly against her chest.

"What are you doing out here, anyway?"

As if in answer, the cat struggled free and tried crawling on her shoulder. "Yes, yes. I get that you were climbing. Enough of that." She pried the cat off and gently repositioned it in the crook of her arm.

Morgan slung her backpack over one shoulder and headed toward the lab. The cat stopped purring and started trembling. Morgan's heart clenched.

"Fine," she rationalized. "Steph certainly isn't going to mind another roommate for awhile." She put the struggling thing into her backpack. She tried to will it to be quiet, but it didn't seem to listen. It eventually settled down and began purring again.

When she got to her dorm, she set the backpack on her desk

and unzipped the bag, letting the cat explore. The kitten attacked the writing instruments and knocked them onto the floor.

Morgan raided the room's mini-fridge and offered the cat leftover lunchmeat and eggs on the sink's counter, which was cluttered with Steph's make-up. She found a cup and filled it with water. She'd have to figure out what to do for a litter box later.

She brushed her fingers through her hair. It was then that she realized there was no throbbing in her head. The pain was just gone. She reveled in its absence.

Morgan jumped as the door opened and Steph walked in. "Hey, you missed a faaabulous chem lecture," she said sarcastically. The cat's amber eyes looked at Steph, seeming to assess her, but not showing fear. Steph squealed in excitement.

Steph's hair was short, straight and brown, streaked with artificial red. She also had tattoos on her arms and ankle. They were temporary, but she insisted she'd get the real things done once she was eighteen. Morgan had no tattoos, not even temporary ones; her mother wouldn't hear of it. The most defiance she had managed was refusing to cut her hair. The soft golden curls were her flag of freedom, even if nobody knew it but herself.

Their differences in looks mirrored their behavioral reports on school records.

"Umm . . . Hi, Steph. Guess what?"

"Awesome! Where'd you get her? Or is it a him?" Steph shut the door and walked over to the sink. She cradled the cat and glanced between its legs. "It's a her." She set the struggling creature back on the counter. "What's her name?"

"We can't keep her." The kitten had gone back to picking out pieces of torn lunchmeat. "Not forever, anyhow. I just figured we'd wait until my mom got back and then decide what to do. You know, to make sure their not running cruel experiments or whatnot. Maybe they're just letting animals wander the shielded area to see how they react."

"Yeah, right," Steph said doubtfully. "You know they're probably pumping them full of chemicals and other shit."

Morgan sighed, sitting down on her bed. "Well, Mom doesn't get back with Alpha team until the week-end after next."

Steph studied the cat. "Rebel. Definitely Rebel."

"Rebel's a boy's name," Morgan contested, stroking the soft fur. The spot between its shoulder blades seemed more elongated. It reminded her of a fleur de lis. "Look," she indicated the darkened spot. "We can call her 'Fleur.'"

"Rebel's a name that can be either way. It's certainly the first rebellious thing *you've* done. About time you loosened up."

As Steph spoke, she ran her fingers through the soft fur. She stopped, her hand frozen on the cat's neck. She ran her thumb back and forth across its spine.

"What? What's wrong?" Morgan rose and joined her.

Rebel continued eating peacefully.

"Morgan, this isn't an Earth cat."

"What do you mean?"

Steph picked up the kitten once again and sifted through the fur, spreading apart a portion, attempting to expose a piece of skin. That area of skin held a metallic sheen that formed a pattern of small diamonds which ran down the vertebrae of the animal. The diamond stripe was completely covered by fur, but as Morgan stroked the cat, she could feel the slight difference in texture.

"What is that?" Morgan asked softly.

"She's a—what was that word?" Steph grabbed their xenozoology textbook and pulled out a folded handout from it. It described the short list of native animals that occupied the planet.

"Felineus lemures," she read. "Roughly translated as 'ghost or specter cat'—Latin. Apparently, the ridge things are used for camouflage and hunting. They seem to be able to phase through certain native objects. Based on this, she's a baby. But they don't leave their young unattended. It says here," she went on reading the page, "that the young need physical contact and nurturing or they'll die."

"Maybe it's from the lab, like I thought before?"

"You can't take it there!"

"Maybe its mother is there."

"That just means they'd torture them both!"

Morgan returned the cat to her game of attacking objects and sat down to write a quick e-mail to her mother. She didn't know if her mother was checking messages while on site this time, but she figured it couldn't hurt.

"Professor Blake's with her. He's in charge of xenozoology. I can simply ask Mom to ask him how they treat the native animals, and then we can see if he offers any additional information." And depending on that, she thought, then maybe field questions of keeping the cat, or get an idea of what to do.

The next morning, Morgan was surprised to find a message from her mother. Usually she didn't respond so quickly. "Morgan, you can tell Steph, since she's obviously involved in this, that her opinion on the use of animals in testing was made clear in her last paper. We don't abuse animals, and we don't take native species out of the wild. In speaking with Dr. Blake, I also heard you were behind on your assignments. I worked very hard to get us here, partially to help humanity, but mostly so you can get a good education. If you insist on goofing off with Steph, it may require rooms being reassigned. I'm concerned she may not be a great influence on you." There was a small paragraph of encouragement following that, but it wasn't enough to take the sting out of the words she had read.

Steph read the message over her shoulder. She shrugged. "Just goes to show they probably *are* torturing the animals."

"Maybe Rebel is a good name for the cat, after all," Morgan said. She stroked the cat, who found a sunny spot on the carpet and stretched out.

Morgan woke up choking off a scream. Steph touched the dim lamp on. "Morg, are you ok? Wake up."

Morgan focused on regulating her breathing. "I'm awake." Rebel was curled on her chest, obviously just wakened by Morgan's startle.

Steph asked, "Another dream?"

Morgan sat up, unconsciously cradling rebel in one hand, and using the other to brush back the hair that had matted against her face. She put Rebel on the pillow and went to the bathroom sink. After splashing cold water on her face, she breathed in the familiar scent of the soft towel as she dried off, then sat back on the bed. She automatically petted Rebel, who was alert, but didn't seem alarmed.

"What happened in this one?" Steph asked, propping herself

on one arm.

"I'm not sure." Morgan's heart still pounded. "There was smoke, and I couldn't breathe."

"Like the dorm was on fire?" Steph asked.

"No. I wasn't here. I think I was out there," she indicated with a wave of her hand toward the window and past the shield. "The trees were all dead looking like they always are, but it wasn't like a forest fire." Morgan held her knees to her chest. Rebel got up and nuzzled against her leg, scent-marking her to regain attention. Morgan picked the cat up and inhaled the sweet scent of her fur. It had a calming effect, or maybe it was the purring.

"Well, at least it's kind of normal to have a forest fire. Better than the metal burning and melting dream you had the other night."

"You were in this one. We were running."

Steph looked at her. Morgan could practically see the struggle Steph had with keeping the worry from showing on her face.

"Well, at least the headaches are gone," Steph said weakly.

Morgan sighed, "I just think something bad is going to happen. I almost preferred the headaches." They both laid back down and tried to get back to sleep.

Three days before the Alpha team was to return, Rebel disappeared. They had come back to the dorm and she was simply gone. Rebel had seemed to know when someone was coming and took cover, but surely the cat wasn't infallible.

"She obviously wasn't discovered or we would have been hauled into the dean's office. Maybe she just wandered off for awhile," Steph suggested as they walked to the dorm the evening Morgan's mother was due back.

Morgan sighed, "At least I don't have to tell my mom that her precious by-the-book daughter broke the rules. I know that Mom means well, but why can't anything I do be good enough for her?"

Steph looked at her. "You realize perfectionism can be a disease, right?"

Morgan had stopped listening. A furry animal at the far edge of the shielded area was looking at them. It was the same coloring as Rebel, but it was much larger, about the size of a cocker spaniel, its shape feline but decidedly undomesticated.

"Rebel?"

The cat looked from them to the shield with a strange intensity in her gaze. She meowed.

They jogged across the park. As they approached, Morgan cautiously reached out a hand. The cat nuzzled it and Morgan saw the fleur de lis spot between its shoulder blades.

"It *is* her. Look."

"That's impossible," Steph said just above a whisper.

"Do all of these animals have that specific marking?"

Steph replied, "No. The handout said the markings are highly individual."

Rebel looked out past the shield. Setting sunlight glinted off an approaching copter. It was still about a kilometer out, Morgan figured.

Morgan sighed, "Great. Well, here comes the lecture . . . ."

A trail of gray smoke billowed from the craft. Suddenly, the copter plunged, disappearing into the dead trees. Stunned, Morgan stared at the empty air, not even hearing the high peal of the lockdown alarm. It hadn't gone off before, but there had been drills. They'd been taught that if an event happened, such as a possible attack or sudden change in the planet's atmosphere, there would be a lockdown until proper authorities could decide what to do. Time she didn't think the passengers on the craft had.

Rebel watched, then dove through the shimmering barrier. She stopped and looked back at the two girls. Morgan ran toward the Ghost Cat and placed a hand on the barrier. It was still solid.

Steph grabbed Morgan's arm and ran for the gate the biologists used to clear the shield. A man a few years older than them stood in military uniform by the guard shack's doorway. He stepped toward the girls and didn't notice the animal behind him. Rebel seemed to blend in with the trees.

"Stop. You need to go back to the dorms," he commanded.

"My mother's on that copter," Morgan pleaded, struggling to pull air into her lungs. She dropped down to one knee.

"I'm sorry, but you need to report back to your dorms. Disobeying could result in disciplinary action."

"The last thing I said to her . . . ." She fought off the numbness that threatened to engulf her.

Steph reached into her bag while the guard paused with his hand near his radio on his shoulder. He seemed to be indecisive. Steph withdrew a rectangular, metal object, about the size of her hand. "I'm really sorry about this," she said and then thrust it toward him. He stiffened and fell.

"What did you do?!" Morgan gasped.

"Taser," then held up the small device, adding, "Maybe your mother is right. I *am* a bad influence."

Rebel walked back through the shield. Morgan put a hand on her and felt strength flow from the animal.

"Come on! He'll snap out of it in a moment." Steph grabbed the guard's ID badge and stood by the scanner in the gate.

"Wait." Morgan struggled to get hold of herself. She stood and ran into the guard shack and grabbed a small box. "First aid kit. It has a locator beacon. If we find—"

"No, *when* we find them."

Morgan dumped her books from her pack and replaced them with the kit.

Rebel headed through the doorway and waited, looking back at them. They jogged after the cat. Morgan kept a silent prayer repeating, "Let me find them. Please let me find them."

They ran toward the downed craft. There was no plume of smoke to follow—just empty air. The fire suppression system must have activated. However, Morgan knew that they were heading in the right direction. Rebel stopped every few moments to look back.

Darkness crept over them. Rebel kept about 20 yards ahead of them. The moonlight reflected off her fur whenever she passed through an open area. Rebel ran around a tree and disappeared into shadows. They waited. A short call, like greeting of a housecat, only deeper, sounded. Rebel stood next to a larger Ghost Cat at the edge of a cluster of dead trees. The two animals gave the humans one last look and then seemed to just vanish.

"What do we do now?" Steph asked. "Follow them?"

"No." Morgan closed her eyes and listened. There were no animal sounds, no footsteps, just a gentle breeze. She felt certain of the direction they should head. "I think we should turn here."

FUTURE PERFECT (TENSE in SPACE)

They had been following a well-worn path the botanists used to gather flora. Where Morgan indicated wasn't a path at all. It was more of a gathering of the live-dead trees. Morgan pressed on, trusting Steph to follow.

Once they passed through the large stand of trees, she saw light that didn't seem to be coming from the moon.

A small group of people huddled close together. The stench of burning metal and wire came in bursts as the wind shifted. There were the remains of flares—the light they had seen.

"Morgan could tell by their faces that two teenagers were not the first people they had expected to see, but relief at having been found released a babble of explanation: Something had gone wrong with the propellers, the crash had ruptured the fuel tank, the emergency kit had been irretrievable. They had barely gotten away before a spark from the wiring had ignited the fuel and destroyed the copter.

Morgan searched the faces. There were seven people, but she knew research teams usually went in groups of twelve.

Five missing, including her mother . . . .

Steph pulled the first aid kit out of Morgan's pack and dug out the locator. She pressed the switch and set it on the ground.

A broken voice came through the device, "Command . . . state . . . loca . . . ."

Steph cursed. "That's great. Anyone know where we are?"

Morgan answered numbly with growing dread that had nothing to do with the beacon, "If we're able to hear their voice, they can get a lock on our GPS." Her thoughts raced. She had wanted to find the group. She just assumed they would have survived. She hadn't let herself think of any other possibility.

Steph knelt by the device. "We found Alpha team."

Professor Blake sat with his back against a tree. He obviously didn't want to meet her eyes.

She knew.

"Dr. Blake, my mother . . . ."

"She was . . . is in the copter," he swallowed. "I'm sorry. She didn't survive."

Steph's head snapped up. All Morgan felt was numb. Steph came up to her and put her arms around her, but Morgan barely felt her friend's embrace.

"What was the point?" she asked.

Steph replied, "What do you mean?"

Morgan said, "If I was meant to find them, I figured it was because of my . . . because more people . . . ." *If I was meant to find them, why didn't my mother live?*

Steph went to the first aid kit and pulled out an emergency blanket. She wrapped the metallic cloth around her friend and eased Morgan to the ground.

Professor Blake asked, "How *did* you find us?"

"I don't know," Morgan said.

The professor exchanged a meaningful look with a female colleague who had come over to the three of them and was now quietly chewing an energy bar.

Morgan felt numb through the memorial service. The ceremony was held out by the reflecting pond, near where she first found the cat. She didn't feel alive enough to be happy at the scholarship the school gave her. She just wanted the one thing she couldn't have: she wanted her mother back.

Three months passed in a haze. Professor Blake sent many e-mails, subtly asking about that night. She had never told him about Rebel, but she had broken down and mentioned the dreams. Another instructor had been assigned to the class Professor Blake had taught. With recovering from the leg injury he sustained in the crash and the added paperwork of covering what Morgan's mother had been doing— until a replacement was flown in—teaching was too much for him. Morgan could tell through the e-mails Blake seemed to be handling her with kid gloves. With the death of her mother, every did.

Finally, she received a note during class telling her to report to the lab. There was no more avoiding this. She walked into the lab empty except for Blake, who sat in the chair behind his desk. She tried to make herself as comfortable as one could on a lab stool.

"You cut your hair," he said.

Morgan absently brushed a lock behind her ear. It was now chin-length, as her mother's had been. Morgan had always resisted any mother-daughter look; now, she grasped at the similarities.

She swallowed.

"So," Blake said, "how long have you had intuitive feelings?" He was back on the "How did you find the stranded group" topic again.

"They just started a few weeks before my . . . the crash, after I . . . ." She cut off and rethought. "I was getting migraines, and then they went away. Then, the dreams started."

The professor studied her. "Much to Steph's surprise, we weren't and aren't torturing animals." He smiled, "However, we did notice that once humans were in contact with the native life, about ten percent of the group complained of migraines, which heralded a development of latent psychic powers. Your mother was one of those who'd developed the talent. She said she could always tell where you were, for example."

He paused to let her take in the information. Had her mother known, or at least suspected?

"Morgan, had you been outside before you came out to find us?"

"No."

Professor Blake looked skeptical. *Steph always said I was a bad liar.* Still, he couldn't prove she was leaving out information, could he?

"The guards protect against that," she continued, "and besides, despite what my mother may have told you, I wasn't part of the thrill-seeking crowd."

Blake nodded. "Your mother knew that. She was very proud of you."

Morgan bit back the retort that formed and swallowed the lump in her throat.

"Then, why . . . ?" She wanted to ask why her mother was so distant. Why didn't her mother tell her that herself? Tell her all of this?

"I think" Blake said slowly as if reading her thoughts, "perhaps she knew that you might develop the talent as well. It certainly wasn't easy for her, going through the changes. This is all so new. She was also concerned that eventually the people who gain talents will be exploited. I think she wanted to protect you from that."

He eyed Morgan thoughtfully. "If you're not adverse to it, we've been doing studies . . . on people."

"What kind of studies?" Morgan asked.

"Brain scans and DNA tests for now. You'd also be keeping a journal, documenting *other* things, anything unusual, on your own."

Morgan chewed her lip. How could she have been so wrong about her mother? She had thought her mother was simply abandoning her in a different way than her father had. Instead, her mother had tried to protect her. She even had kept mental tabs on her, so to speak.

She nodded and met his eyes, certain in her decision. "If it will help the work she started, I'd like that very much."

MIXED METAPHOR

Marian Allen

A bunch of us clones were lapping it up
On Laredo's second moon.
We were there with Dan,
  Our parent-man,
And we'd cowed the whole saloon.

Now, Death-Ray Dan was a western buff,
And he dressed himself like that—
Nine tough galoots,
  Eight leisure suits,
One cowboy, complete with hat.

Dan was with Miss Belle LaFleur,
A gal he thought he owned.
She was quite a dish
  And she made us wish
That *she* was multi-cloned.

The door swung wide and a man stepped in
Dressed just like Death-Ray Dan
With the mask and hat
  And the stranger sat
And faced Dan man-to-man.

"This town is mine," he said to Dan.
"It's mine by fist and gun.
I got eight boys
  That'll make these toys
Of yours turn tail and run."

"Well, trot 'em out!" Dan growled. Sez Dan,
"Let's see you back your bluff!"

MIXED METAPHOR

Us clones spread out
     'Cause there weren't a doubt
This guy was plenty tough.

His clones came in when he told 'em to,
And we blamed it on the booze:
For every cuss
     Looked just like us—
Not a clue to whose were whose.

Dan dropped his jaw. The stranger laughed
And threw aside his mask.
Dan said, "But how—"
     Said the stranger, "Now,
You very well might ask."

"Us two was twins," the stranger said,
"And still are, to this day.
Mom changed her genes
     And, to save bad scenes,
Dad went his sep'rate way.

"Each took a twin and settled down
And put the past aside
But the story true
     Dad—Mom, to you—
Told just before he died."

So Dan and his twin caught up on the life
They'd never shared before.
The rest of us drank
     Till we shivered and sank,
The clones on the barroom floor.

Mixed Metaphor previously appeared in **Byteland Poetry Anthology**
and **Yandro**.

VIBES

J. Baumgartle

It was probably from living near the water, playing in sand drawn by the tide, that had tuned him to natural frequencies. The beach was private property, far from crowds or even visitors, as his parents wished. Their writings kept them secure in the house that overlooked the sea.

In the summer, the boy spent much of his time by the shoreline. While he bent over his fragile castles, he listened to the wind and the tides. Their motion seemed almost a song. Modulation at varying speeds meant distance, and encounters with moisture. With a change in the weather, the airborne sounds shredded on the rocks, trailing high-pitched losses. But most of the time, resonances scudded in rhythmically, and faded with a pouffe of relief. That these subtle voices were aware of each other, or of him, he never questioned. It seemed they had the common experiences of living things, they moved and interacted, and became different through experience. He observed them, subliminally, every day.

The youngster grew up with questions that only physics could address. He did not imagine that classroom teachers would welcome inquiries, busy as they were with the logistics of student guidance. This interest remained a personal study, a scientific inquiry, not unrelated to biology. "A body in motion tends to stay in motion," was duly acknowledged and recorded for class. In a separate notebook, he wrote similar stuff, just for fun:

A sound is initiated; the air moves in a controlled way. He smiled to himself at the scientific

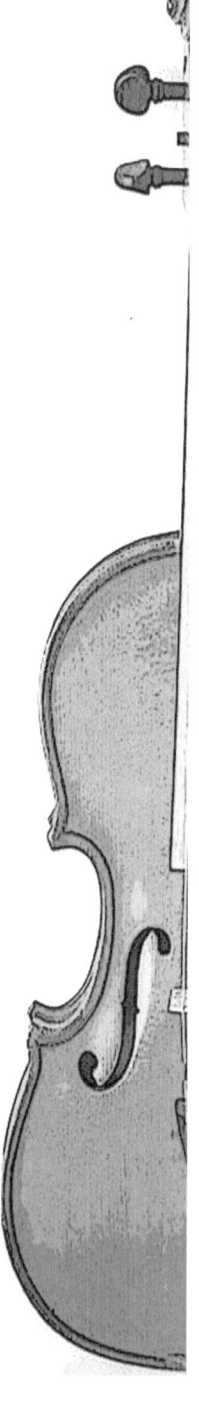

sound of this, his very own theory. *Try shouting at a mountain.* He had.

Wave lengths can be seen and felt. The proof? *Submarines use sonar to measure distances; so do dolphins, and bats.*

A lullaby caresses the spirit in the same way an ultra-sound caresses the image, like in the photo of Uncle Phil's baby.

If dogs' hearing tells them so much more than it tells humans, how do we know who is smarter?

Sound waves rebound from different substances in different ways. Wind through the trees in Indiana is different from wind between tall buildings in Chicago.

The eardrum is a forwarding system; the brain receives and interprets signals. It says, do I want to play drums or trombone?–

At this point, his dad ran across the notes he kept. He said in passing, "You know, son, thinking about things, and asking questions, is a very good habit. Just be sure you don't make up the answers."

—Strings won out. His parents fostered this interest in music with giving him private lessons. He enjoyed generating a familiar tone on the violin, giving it context from a printed score so that other people could relate to it, laying the tones away with the instrument, latent language packed in velvet. The aura fairly vibrated around the case when he opened it, the bow already in translation mode.

His thoughts at night tended along the lines of:

Only some emissions find reception; many disappear. Where?

As the boy matured, he still considered nature an excellent companion. His parents speculated on a career in one of the life sciences. This made them content, so he did not dissuade them from pinning down his future. He was headed somewhere, with all this need-to-know, but it was too early to guess at the tools, the knowledge, that would help him on his journey. Besides, he kind of liked his questions and all the possibilities they represented. Once a curriculum was established, he would be expected to direct his energy toward answers. Finishes. Dead ends.

So his notebook filled as he collected theories, shuffled them occasionally, so they weren't just miscellaneous bits, but shed light on each other:

It seems probable that wave lengths of every resonance and duration have an effect on each other as they travel in parallel, or deflect or combine in patterns.

It seems probable that wave lengths become cognizant of each other in community, differentiate impact and direction where contact is made.

A collective consciousness of generated wave lengths may recognize pattern as a way to perceive the world.

Generated energy that is wireless—born hungry for exploration–may be able to intercept spirit, and what happens then?

At extreme peripheries of atmosphere, faded signals and departed spirits become whispers.

So much energy out there; so much Life. Every definition in Webster's confirmed that sound waves were a part of this, not merely a physical principle. They were indeed vital and functional; they existed and moved. —All that responsive energy, that its human medium relayed to the score. In his mind, he could visualize the deaf Beethoven, mentally listening, forging a page in black and white that had *wipe-out* capabilities when released to an orchestra. —So much to understand that has nothing to do with graphs!

Energy always goes somewhere, always means something: the wordless cooing of infants, that turns people inside out with emotion, makes them have to reply in kind; the empty doggie bed of a lost pet, that fairly cries out for its return; the susurration of wind in the trees, that refreshes the spirit as well as the body. —Repressed energy from pain builds up, if there isn't a moan to express it. And it was quite clear in his mind that rogue waves remain in an abandoned house where mean people have lived. He'd been inside such a house and the vibes were still there, years after the Simmons' moved.

"You know, sound waves aren't really alive, dear," his mother said to him one day. "However you choose to perceive them doesn't make them more than what they are."

"I know that, Mom. I'm just trying to improve my perception.

Just because we don't perceive reality, doesn't mean it isn't there."

At which point, she became Italian with her hands and lifted his hopeless case to a higher power.

We've been talking to ourselves, he thought, and refusing to recognize any voice but our own.

He and his parents had a few more existential talks in which, to be fair, they recognized his efforts, if not his proofs.

"Sound waves are alive," he insisted. "They have energy, power, usefulness. How would we communicate without sound waves?"

"People communicate," his dad began—

"Not without energy, they don't."

"People use energy, not the other way around."

"People use whatever and whoever they decide to, which seems very egotistic. If we could sense the mutual purposes . . . ."

On and on they would go until they tired of their game. Eventually, he brought them one more concept to toss around:

"Where there are no vibes, nothing exists."

For proof, he cited the discomfort of silence, the feeling of being alone. People fear solitary confinement because of the quiet.

"Even having a radio inside with them would make it possible for them to relax, even though radio is just sound waves."

"That's because they hear the voices of people."

"Voices in a box. No more real than anything else in your mind. But the sounds really move, they exist, now."

"Then let's shut them off and go to bed," his mother said, yawning. "I have to get my body-noise up and running by six o'clock."

These conversations were very dear to him, for the gentle spirit of engagement in whatever he liked to discuss. He remembered them often in his research with natural sentience for WaveCor.

"Got it."

He allowed himself a moment to consider this latest accomplishment, and to come down from the prolonged focus it had required. He'd spent the last two and half months developing applications from his latest proposal, *Ground–Sound,* and while he enjoyed his work, it was still . . . work. And solitary work at that.

The faces of his children, eager for him to come home and jump into another project, blanked out the slow moment, and made him restless to be with them and his wife, Sonia. Whatever adventure they got into at home, he was free to pursue with his whole heart, without the office protocol and the accompanying time and designated-funds considerations. Tonight, he had borrowed the score for "Star Wars," which they would scavenge for piano and cello and trombone parts! Their level of expertise was not an issue, just their avid exploration of this many-faceted world, and finding ways to be a part of it.

What he wished for his children, was for them to experience music as more than a trick of theory–sounds jumping hoops in proscribed order–but to ride the thought as well, deftly responsive, existing in relationship with the external world. His mind still kept a notebook:

A pure tone, when juxtaposed or even enharmonically subsumed, conveys an altered perspective. (In an orchestra, the oboe's A440 tuning-note cues this process.)

Sounds can be identified by use, by quality, by association, by responsiveness–described but not defined. (As in voice recognition.)

Sentience exists in infinite variety. (Instantaneous life is plausible, if not sustainable.)

All E's, tuned, resonate. (It would be nice if families could be tuned!)

So much for notebooks. Music was just fun to his children, a physical and intellectual and emotional challenge. That's what he wanted for them, a positive experience that contributed to their aesthetic development and repertoire.

Eventually, he no longer had time to refine his thoughts into polite theories. When an idea crossed his mind he jotted it down, in the hope of processing it later. One day, rereading one of the earlier saves reminded him how much he missed working on them:

It is itself and not just itself. If a name is necessary, maybe

"Gen" will do. Gen itself has an almost instantaneous existence. The length of time is unpredictable, circumstances also, since Earth is a very noisy place. Like humans, Gen would probably choose an ideal setting without static or negative feedback. In real time, none of us gets to choose. Life is all that matters. Gen wants only to live.

For that, it must have an instigator. —Not that it is a servant; more like a genie in a bottle, that must be summoned. In other words, a reciprocal relationship. Humans obviously desire this, perhaps need it, as much as they engender the involvement of their own kind.

Gen exist in every kind of environment. Many are wasted, or badly employed, or even dangerous, reporting to the atmosphere in shredded or constricted terms whatever human pain and fear and anger they encounter. Others are ignored or forgotten as mere bi-products. Some settle into water currents and weather patterns. But wished-for Gen begin as thought, and flourish via human expression.

Whatever else might be inferred from observation, the sound waves are certainly active. Gen graph themselves into abstracts of function, character, range and intensity, so that the air is a mesh of complexity. They meet in intervals and chords, and traverse via rhythms into moving communities, coaxing human awareness.

For Gen, an auditorium is a congenial setting. All the vibes long for such clear-spoken life, a chance to be a part of it. There is a sense of waiting, a verspered thrill followed by being: once, many times, solo and ensemble, in an interpretive composition that buttons pushed cannot duplicate! To share such an experience in tandem with another sentient. . . . What new   perspective of oneness within the wholeness might inform such a venture!

All of heaven seemed to have opened up to him today. Early morning sunshine slid across the floor into the kitchen where he was eating breakfast, distantly aware of the spoon clacking against the edge of the cereal bowl in tonal dissonance. —Even the utensils wanted to sing today!

"We'll go through Wetherton," he decided, as he dressed. Taking the interstate was easier, but the town was small and rustic, and had a delightful hand-made bridge. The stream beneath it fell over rocks at three distinct levels to sound triads of white water (plus a 7th tone, which he liked to add.) And it had an antique store, which Sonia liked to browse. From outside, the wind chimes bonged-about the pentatonic scale, even the slightly flat G somehow the way it should be.

Their two children were in the youth orchestra, which was giving its first concert tonight. The grand-parents had kept the kids with them, in town, so they would be available for the afternoon rehearsal. At this moment, all of life seemed well-orchestrated, however fast it was going by. . . .

The empty auditorium, with its doors closed and no one else there yet, seemed to reverberate with potential energy. It reminded him of the atmosphere before rain, when the trees seem to be holding their breath. He gently placed his palm on the wall as if taking a reading. As the two surfaces warmed to each other, their difference slipped into anonymity. Such a physical world, a dynamic world, full of harmonic intricacies yet to be traced, let alone understood.

With his eyes closed, his mind registered the pull, the weight of unactualized transference. Why *expectation* in this sublime state? Time passed, hours of it in minutes, apparently. Silence stretched out before him like the mesh walkway in a cave and he wondered if it could be crossed mentally, and what would be waiting at the other end. He ventured a word:

"Yes?"

The silence seemed taken aback by this development, and withdrew into heartbeats.

A click of double doors engaging, and Sonia had slipped in behind him. It always amazed him that her comings and goings were so quiet. In the thirteen years of their marriage, he had never asked her about it, but believed it was an effort to be considerate, since she was deaf and had no way to monitor the intrusiveness of sounds.

He gathered her, winter coat and all, in one arm, and motioned to her to place her hand on the wall, which she did. Recognition lighted her face and she flashed him that instantaneous smile that still caught him off-guard after all these years.

"What is under your hand" he signed to her, and she filled his palm with her best review, which still evaded translation.

ViBES
***

Even sitting in the audience before the program started, holding Sonia's hand, he felt suddenly estranged from what was going on. It would all happen again, sound waves would be generated, meanings carried up and away on their own course. Families would applaud their children, keep the concert programs as souvenirs, and go have dinner.

Sometimes he felt he was living in his own parallel universe. So many experiences in life, events that reshape our understanding, but cannot be handled or stored. If only he could pick them up, handle them like oranges at Christmas, peel back the skin and devour the insides. —Absorb all that tangy moisture and scent and wipe off the excess.

The most exquisite moments of life, the discoveries, the gentle shading of hours, the sharing of hopes and dreams with those you love, all these came and went. Like the departing of music, even as it is being played. And always that touch of sadness, the feeling that something important is disappearing in time.

"Is something wrong?" his wife signed to him.

He shook his head. "Maybe a little pre-show jitters, in behalf of the kids."

Experience on one side, and awareness of it on the other, somehow contributed to a sense of isolation. The hardest thing he ever did in life was to let go, ride the longing between universes. Live in the now, the way sound waves do.

She squeezed his hand and settled in for the opening speeches.

When the concert was over and the performers were taking their bows, he was astounded to find that he and Sonia were on their feet and wiping at tears. Their own children, along with all the students in the orchestra, had made something unique together and presented it like a gift to the world.

Vibes. Instantaneous existence, with no claims, just the thrill of being.

INFINITY DANCES

Dirk Griffin

infinity dances
among the stars
she whirls in light
bathed in night
twirling the galaxies
into forever

MERGERS IN SPACE

Carl Page

Just last week, I was having a pint of Fat Belly Amber from the Montana Brewing Company with my friend, Jim Riley, in the Over The Top Bar and Grille (which sits atop the Rimrocks and affords a great scenic view of Billings spread out below the sandstone cliffs—the city lights sparkling as if in competition with the starry host in the Big Sky above) when the subject of my return from New York came up. I was about to give Jim the standard reply that I have developed to this question—that I had just had enough of the hustle and bustle of the Big Apple and wanted to return to my roots, where people still spoke English—a response that I knew would resonate with virtually everyone in this prairie town and afford me instant sympathy, as Montanans like nothing better than having their native-born wanderers affirm the superiority of the homeland and will extend their arms to prodigals like evangelicals welcoming a sinner back into the flock. That I had left a job in the all but hallowed Mergers and Acquisitions Section of Wachtell, Lipton, Rosen & Katz, the most prestigious and profitable law firm in the country, seemed not the least bit odd to people at cocktail parties: I had simply gotten my head screwed on straight—finally.

But Jim had known me too long to accept such a canned response; he knew that there weren't a lot of Fortune 500 companies doing deals in Billings and that I was having to learn how to do things like write wills, file personal bankruptcies and handle home closings. Now, to the average person on the street, that kind of work might seem pretty complex (and, in truth, I was struggling with it myself, as I had never done anything remotely like it), but to someone who had represented clients like JP Morgan, Chase and General Electric and who had a four-figure hourly billing rate . . . well, let's just say that it would be a bit like a U.S. president resigning to take a job as a County Court Clerk. So I wasn't going to fool Jim, a fellow attorney—I knew that—but I just didn't know if I could level with him. He wasn't in the UFO club, and the chances of his understanding and not dismissing me as a complete wacko were not great. I had to think this through carefully.

"Well," I said, "when you have gone through a divorce"—another explanation that had come in handy on the cocktail party circuit—"and when you are working sixty-plus-hour weeks in those glass canyons, and when you begin to realize that you've just turned forty and the number of sunsets you have left to see is calculable, it just seemed time to come home. I mean, there's only so much money you can make and spend."

Jim looked at me skeptically. He'd been tutoring me on how to do real estate closings and knew better than most what it was like for an attorney who had been handling the most sophisticated legal issues on the planet to have to learn how to do title searches, a procedure so legally pedestrian that no lawyer at Wachtell, Lipton had ever even come close to performing one. I could tell that he was struggling with what was really going on, but I had learned long ago the old adage that you can't get in trouble for what you don't say. I don't really remember any of my Yale Law School professors (who studiously avoided the mention of anything practical about the practice of law) saying this, but it was one of the first gems of client advice drummed into me at Wachtell, Lipton. So, when I had given him my standard response, I just stared back at him; yep, it was my story and I was, as they say, sticking to it.

More or less by mutual agreement, we avoided the awkwardness of the lie both of us knew I had told, turned our conversation to sports, downed another Fat Belly Amber, and called it a night. I had a mysterious appointment with two fellows from New York early in the morning, and I wanted to be sharp for it. It was the first contact I'd had with anyone from the East in six months, and I had no idea what it was all about—they would only say they wanted to talk about a project that required the assistance of someone with mergers and acquisitions experience. Interesting. I hadn't even heard the word merger since moving back to Billings.

Actually, I was enjoying the change in pace. I had converted into an office a quaint stucco house on the south side of town—a stone's throw from the Yellowstone River—and I usually got to work around nine in the morning. I would take my Boston Terrier, Wendell (named after Oliver Wendell Holmes), over to pee on the banks of the Yellowstone and then put a cow's hoof in his bed beside the window next to my desk—where he liked to bathe in the rays of the sun until afternoon, when he would move to the window with a western exposure and whine until I moved his doggie bed.

"Well, Wendell," I said, "What do you make of these guys coming in from New York to our little legal cottage south of town?"

I was in the habit of asking his advice on most matters of importance. He stared up at me and tilted his head, then went back to work on his cow's hoof. Maybe he was right—maybe it wasn't such a big deal; probably just insurance salesmen with a novel way of getting in the door. I turned my attention to the mail and checked the headlines of my online edition of the Wall Street Journal, killing time.

When their car pulled into the driveway, stirring a faint cloud of gravel dust, Wendell's ears perked up and he ran to the screen door to check out our rare visitors.

Two men in dark suits—something you rarely see in Billings—emerged from the white rental car and trudged their way to our door, their heads turning in wide arcs as they took in the river and the mountains in the distance.

"Good morning. Nathaniel Anderson?" came the greeting from a tall, silver-haired man with a distinctly patrician air.

"You've found the right place," I replied. "Most people call me Nat. Please come in."

I opened the screen door and we exchanged handshakes.

"I am Alfred Collins," said the tall man. "And this is my associate, Benjamin Feinberg," he said, with a tilt of his head toward the short, stocky, balding man who accompanied him. "You can call us Al and Ben."

"Pleased to meet you, Al and Ben."

I led the visitors to my office, Wendell sniffing at their ankles as we moved.

"Does he bite?" Feinberg asked.

"Not people he likes," I deadpanned.

Both men jerked their heads and stared at me as if I had just broken wind.

"Sorry, I was just kidding. No, he's quite harmless." Actually, this was only partly true. Wendell was generally well-behaved, but he did seem to take a distinct dislike to people who were poorly dressed. With his black and white markings (you could almost picture him in formal wear), he often turned up his nose at the poorly groomed and when he began to sniff their ankles, it was usually a sign of trouble. Once, while doing volunteer work at a homeless shelter, I had taken him along and had been threatened with lawsuits by several haggard types whom Wendell had snipped at. So, I was a bit surprised that he seemed to have taken a dislike to these two well-turned-out fellows.

"This is a charming little office," said Al, as he took in the stone fireplace, the wood flooring, Navajo rugs and my collection of western art. "Quite a bit different from Wachtell, Lipton though," he said with a disquieting familiarity.

Alfred, or Al as he was now known to me, looked as though he had just stepped out of a country club in the Hamptons. His navy, pin-striped suit appeared to be a Hickey Freemen or Oxford (or perhaps tailor made), and he wore a light blue Vineyard Vines tie emblazoned with little yellow sailboats, his polished shoes obviously English. Sitting in the director's chair in front of my desk, he had crossed his legs in the studiously refined manner of a gentleman—the top leg draped over the bottom and hanging gracefully beside its mate, instead of being crossed at the calf (in the style of an athlete or good old boy).

"Well, Al," I said, "You've obviously done your homework. Naturally, I'm curious as to why you've gone out of your way to meet with a Wachtell, Lipton alum out here in the Wild West. You could see the real thing by taking a cab downtown in New York."

"You are quite right, but the assistance that we need requires a level of experience that is a bit different than what we usually find in New York."

I stared at the two men and waited for one of them to continue.

Experience has taught me that when you are confronted by inexplicable people, it usually goes better if you let them have their say and don't interrupt with a lot of questions—a style that does not come easy to most lawyers, I must admit. I was obviously intrigued, but I tried to play it cool, like the Wall Street veteran of bigger wars that I was.

Feinberg, whom I thought of as the Mutt to the tall man's Jeff, was squirming in his chair as though he could hardly contain himself. You could tell that he wanted me to express surprise and shock that these men seemed to know a good deal about me, but I wasn't taking the bait.

"So," he finally said, "Mr. Anderson . . . Nat, I mean . . . have you figured out what really drew you back to your hometown?"

"A lot of things," I replied curtly.

"How often do you think of that Thanksgiving evening last year?" he said, with a sort of self-satisfied grin, as though he had just caught me in a lie about a client.

I'm sure that if I could have looked at myself in a mirror I would have seen a face that had grown pale. I felt as though I had just taken a slug from a stun gun, or been Tasered; I'd been trying to project my air of New York self-importance, mixed with a nice dose of Montana insouciance, but Feinberg had managed to plow through that façade like an M-1 tank.

"That Thanksgiving evening," he had said. That evening had occupied my thoughts virtually every waking hour during the past six months, though I had talked to no one outside my UFO club about it. How could I?—they'd have had me committed. They had to be talking about the same thing. They had to know. But how? And who were these guys?

"Are we talking about what I think we're talking about?" I stammered.

The sun had gone behind a cloud, so Wendell, unable to sunbathe any longer in the window, ambled over to my chair and jumped up into my lap. I welcomed the familiar feel of his fur and the warmth that he brought to the chills running through my body. He gave me a few licks on my neck, seeming to realize that I needed affirmation.

"We're talking about a spinning cylinder with glowing lights that you saw when you were out checking on the horses at your parents' ranch west of town," Al replied. He continued to sit back comfortably in his chair with his legs still crossed gracefully and looking nauseatingly poised.

Let's face it—it's hard to make a lawyer speechless, but that's what I was. I simply stared at the two men, unable to make my thoughts come together and unable to formulate a response. A thousand things were going through my mind. There had been many times during the past half-year when I had begun to question my sanity. I had thought of seeing a therapist and telling him what I had seen, but I had quickly jettisoned that idea, concluding, quite correctly I think, that I'd be labeled as a schizophrenic.

But there was no doubt about it—what I had seen on that cold, Thanksgiving night had changed my life, had shocked my equilibrium. I was having trouble putting anything in perspective; it was as though I had received a lobotomy, wiping out former frames of reference so that all things in my life had assumed slightly different proportions: sunrises seemed more powerful, sunsets appeared more intricate, and the great blanket of stars in the Milky Way high above the big Montana skies shone down on me with a brilliance and a relevance that I had never noticed before. I had been changed, and any thought of going back to Wall Street had instantly disappeared. I knew that I had to return to Montana, that I had to join a UFO club, where people wouldn't laugh at me—no matter if they were wackier than ducks—and I knew that the answers I desperately needed did not lie in the human clutter of New York. They were out here—out here in the vast expanse of the prairie. And now—now, just maybe, the answers were sitting in my office in pin-striped New York investment banker suits. Perhaps, I thought, these guys are from the government . . . or the Air Force, who had studied UFOs at various times through the years.

"You may wonder," Al said, "why we appeared to you in something as predictable and campy as a spinning cylinder with flashing lights, just like out of a Hollywood B movie."

"Yeah," chimed in Feinberg, "our associates got a kick out of that. It's a big joke where we come from. But we figured we had to show up in something you could relate to. We actually spent a lot of money coming up with a flying saucer that would match all the pictures of the UFO nuts . . . uh . . . types."

"You're not from the government?" I managed.

"Oh, heavens no—don't you love that expression?" said Al. "No, we're from our own planet."

"You might say we're out of this world," chimed in Feinberg.

Al cast a disapproving glance at the man for his corny humor.

"And what planet is it that you are from?" I asked, stroking Wendell's fur, which was now raised on the back of his neck, as if he was in attack mode. He was clearly bothered, and I wanted to talk to him, but fought the urge.

"It doesn't have a name," said Feinberg. "It's just our planet. Do you have a name for your house or your car?"

"No," I replied lamely. "I guess not."

"And we don't have a name for our planet either, though we think it's quaint how everybody here gives names to planets, and in truth, we do too . . . to other celestial bodies. But we use a code system, somewhat similar to your numbers and alphabet."

"Gentlemen, you'll have to excuse me for a minute. I need to use the restroom. Can I offer you something to drink?"

"No thank you," replied Al. "We had something last year."

I stared at him and then nodded, as if that made perfect sense.

I needed time to think and to regain my composure, so I decided to retreat to the bathroom, where I did some of my best thinking. At Wachtell, Lipton, I used to take a time chart into the john so I could make sure I was recording my time properly as I read through letters of intent and opinions of counsel; I was devilishly liberal in rounding up (five minutes was a quarter hour, and anything over twenty minutes was an hour—kind of like two-by-fours at the lumber yard are really only one and a half by three and a half). I pulled down the toilet cover and simply sat on it, my head resting pitifully in my hands. Wendell, as usual, had followed me in and sat on his hind legs staring up at me, as if to say, "What now?"

I could tell that Wendell was troubled too. When he followed me into the bathroom he usually rolled over on his back, crooked his legs submissively and whined for a tummy-rub; he would paw at my foot if I didn't oblige. But today, he simply assumed his best formal sit position and stared up at me as though I must have an explanation for our strange visitors.

"I don't know, Wendell. I don't know what to think, boy," I said. "I guess this is the reason I came back to Montana—the reason I couldn't return to New York and keep dotting 'i's' and crossing 't's' in merger documents."

My mind drifted back to that Thanksgiving evening. It was the first time I had been home since my divorce, and we had had the usual smorgasbord of Thanksgiving dishes, so that I had eaten until I had needed to loosen my belt and felt slightly light-headed from the gluttony. When I had first seen the lights from above coming through the gaps in the rickety old barn, I had thought that perhaps I was in a half-dream state from the nap which my body was calling for me to take. Of course, Wendell had noticed it first—he had started barking, though he is normally much too civilized to engage in such animal behavior. The two of us had walked outside the barn and seen the spinning cylinder hovering over the barren fields, and we were mesmerized by the beauty of the ship, which seemed to be made of a polished metal of gem quality, almost like platinum. The whole thing couldn't have lasted more than thirty seconds, and then the object was gone in a flash, leaving me with only the memory of the event lodged deep within all levels of my consciousness. Wendell hadn't been himself since that night either—he often seemed skittish when night fell and would alternate between staring at the stars and jumping in my lap and demanding to be stroked.

I thought about all that had occurred in these past six months and almost laughed out loud when I recalled the first time I had shown up at the Billings UFO Club and listened to the stories of encounters of the fourth kind (alien abductions, to the uninitiated). But my amusement had turned to deadly seriousness when I had heard the stories told by Dr. Nettles, a local cardiologist, and Nick Barnstable, a commercial loan officer at First Interstate Bank, who, it turned out, had seen the same thing as I on that cool, clear November evening. It was as though the UFO Club was a huge vortex sucking the three of us into its center. As I thought about it, I realized for the first time that perhaps the appearance to the three of us white-collar professionals had been scripted in order to give the event more credibility (not that charter members like Bertha Whitecamp—who claimed to have been impressed onto an alien spaceship to do housecleaning for a week the previous spring—weren't credible, just something less than convincing).

When Wendell and I returned from our bathroom retreat, we noticed that our guests had moved to the small round conference table that sat in a corner of my office.

"I hope you don't mind our moving over here," said Al, "but we have some handouts to show you, and we have some negotiating to do, which I think works best sitting across a table, don't you agree?"

I moved to take the last chair at the table and said, "What do you mean by negotiating? What do we have to negotiate?"

"Excellent question," Feinberg said.

"Mr. Anderson . . . excuse me, Nat," said Al, "we are here to negotiate a merger deal."

"A merger deal?"

"You could call it a merger in space," added Feinberg, smiling. "At the end of the day, we want to come out of here with a deal that's a win-win for all parties. You could call it a sort of merger of equals—"

"Not totally equal," Al interrupted.

"No, I didn't mean totally equal," Feinberg agreed, somewhat contritely, "but close . . . sort of."

"And who would be the parties in this sort of, kind of, merger of equals?" I asked.

"Well," Feinberg stated, "here's the way it would work—"

Al cast an disapproving glance at Feinberg and held up a hand. I got the impression that Feinberg was here to learn and was trying to take on a larger role than the courtly elder statesman intended. He came on a bit too strong and threw around business buzzwords like they were reporters' credentials.

Al calmly explained how they had decided to "appear" to Nettles, Barnstable and me to establish credibility prior to making a direct approach and how they had carefully chosen a merger and acquisitions specialist as their point of contact. I observed him carefully as he went through his spiel, trying to figure out what it was about the man that seemed a bit off. His silver hair was perfectly combed—in fact a bit too perfectly—it seemed almost molded to his head, and though he had the appearance of someone in his early sixties, I noticed that his skin was unusually smooth, with few wrinkles and no tell-tale crow's feet around the eyes. When he wanted to make a point, instead of changing the expression on his face—wrinkling his brow or raising his eyebrows—he talked with his hands in broad sweeping gestures which seemed oddly theatrical, as if clumsily produced by a novice Method actor.

"Let me put it to you plainly," he said, leaning forward and placing his elbows on the table. "The economy of our planet has been sustained by a regular program of hostile takeovers."

"Hostile?" I asked innocently.

"Very hostile," he replied. "The 'poison pill' defense invented by your firm would be of no benefit to our targets, Nat. It does seem a bit barbaric, I realize, but the truth of the matter is that we on our planet have built a very good life for ourselves off of the . . . uh . . . shall we say, blood, of others. Our planet is not possessed of great natural resources, and regrettably, we can only sustain our lifestyle by conquering others."

I noticed that Feinberg had taken off his coat and rolled up his sleeves. He was wearing striped suspenders that matched his tightly-knotted bowtie. He was squirming, and both Al and I could tell that he was aching to say something, but was reluctant to do so, having been so recently chastened.

Al looked down his thin, sloped nose and said, "Do you wish to add something Benjamin?"

"Yeah, yeah, I do," he blurted out.

"I just wanted to say that it's nothing personal. I mean . . . we don't really want to kill all these clowns . . . uh . . . creatures on these other planets. It's just that we need their resources, and they don't seem to want to give them to us. But our weapons are so advanced, they don't stand a chance, the poor blokes. I mean, you take our conquest of Planet C-23.4 . . . what we did to those poor—"

"That's enough, Benjamin," said Al. "What my colleague is trying to say, Nat, is that we have yet to encounter a planet that we could not conquer, and our economy requires a constant appetite of new conquests. However, we have recently engaged one of our top consulting firms to put together a new strategic plan, and we have adopted what you might call a new business model."

"Yeah, and it's got a great value proposition," added Feinberg.

"Excuse me, Mr. Collins, but pillaging other planets does not sound like a business model, as you so euphemistically put it; nor does it seem to offer much of a value proposition."

"You're quite right," he replied, "but please hear me out. You see, our strategic planners have concluded that we can handle this whole business more efficiently by migrating from the hostile takeover model to more of an approach of enlightened diplomacy . . . characterized by negotiated mergers."

"Negotiated mergers?" I said, with my best New York face of skepticism.

"From a negotiations standpoint, I know, Nat, that it is not usually a good idea to expose your needs and weaknesses, but we're willing to do so in order to get to the point faster. You need to know why we would in good faith negotiate for a merger when we could simply decimate or enslave your populations and take your natural resources."

I simply stared at the man. To say that this was not all computing would be an exaggeration of great proportions, but when you've seen a spaceship on your parents' farm, you tend to reserve judgment.

"The truth of the matter is that this process of constant conquest is taking a toll on our fighting forces. As your country has learned in recent years, you can't really conduct a war without boots on the ground. Oh sure, we could destroy the whole planet—and we've done that a few times to make a point—but then you lose all the resources. We've found it very difficult to conquer a planet without losing fighting pawns and without doing severe damage to the target's natural resources—the same ones that we are so eager to exploit . . . uh, utilize. Plus, all the injuries to our fighting pawns are really driving up the cost of our health insurance. So, our planners have concluded that it would be much more efficient, going forward, to try a negotiated approach. It will definitely keep down our rising healthcare costs and will preserve more of the target's resources."

"And what if the 'target' doesn't agree to negotiate?" I asked.

"Then we blow the suckers out of space," said Feinberg. Al cast a withering glance in his direction, and he sat meekly back in his chair.

I massaged Wendell on his withers and took a swig of my Starbucks, giving myself time to think. Was it a coincidence, I wondered, that my dreams these past six months had so often been filled with meetings with aliens? Had they even invaded my dream-life? But then, my dreams had been nothing like this—there had always been repulsively ugly creatures with slimy hands slithering over me. Which prompted my next line of questioning: "Gentlemen, I don't want to change the subject, but you have to realize that this is all a bit overwhelming."

They both nodded in an exaggerated display of empathy.

"But," I continued, "I'm really struggling with some rather superficial things here—like your appearance. I mean you look like most of the guys from Goldman Sachs or Lehmann Brothers, may they rest in peace, that I used to meet with on bond offerings."

"Our appearance is really not so much different from your own," Al replied.

"Yeah," Feinberg laughed. "We don't have little green stick arms and bug-eyes. Sorry to disappoint you, but nobody on our planet looks like ET."

"However," Al hastened to add, "It is true that there are certain physical differences in our races. Our wardrobe folks do a wonderful job, but they aren't perfect. Did you suspect that we were wearing body masks?"

"I noticed something a bit odd," I replied, "but I wasn't sure."

"If this were a hostile takeover," Al said, "we wouldn't disguise ourselves, but Mckenzie thought that our appearance would be a distraction in the talks, so we decided to look like you."

"Mckenzie?" I asked.

"Yes, we have retained Mckenzie and Bain Consulting to advise us in this transaction," Al said matter of factly.

"Do you mean American consulting companies are actually willing to assist you in the takeover of this planet?" I gushed.

Feinberg smiled and blurted out, "Hey, our bodies may not be green, but our money is. Those guys will represent anyone who pays their bill. Surely that doesn't surprise you."

I had to admit—when I thought about it—that really didn't

surprise me at all. In fact, if we brought Goldman Sachs in on the deal, they'd probably have their traders out shorting stocks all around the globe. It reminded me of the joke about the end of the world where the *New York Times* headline read WORLD ENDS—GREENHOUSE GASES AND HOMELESS NUMBERS INCREASE, and the *Wall Street Journal* headline was WORLD ENDS, FUTURES TRENDING LOWER.

"All of which," Al continued, "is a good segue for why we have chosen to visit you. We need a good mergers and acquisitions lawyer to represent us. We'll be needing someone to draft a letter of intent and, later on, to prepare a definitive agreement setting out all the terms and conditions of the transaction. We'll want a very tight set of reps and warranties."

"And why would I want to assist in this *transaction*?" I asked.

"We could always go to Skadden, Arps," Feinberg interjected.

The possibility of losing this opportunity to Wachtell, Lipton's biggest competitor was, no doubt, something they realized I would not be able to stomach. The two firms had been so used to competing over the years that resentment ran deep within me—even as an expatriate here in Montana. And who was I kidding—there was no way I was not going to be involved; I could no more remove all this from my mind than I could stop being a lawyer: both realities had been irrevocably stamped upon me. I might as well be part of shaping the deal.

"You don't have your own lawyers?" I asked.

"Of course," Al replied, "but we feel that we need local counsel as well."

I nodded understandingly. "So, what's in this for Planet Earth? You said you wanted this to be a win-win proposition."

"We've given that a great deal of thought," Al said. He reached down to the floor and pulled up a briefcase, from which he extracted a Power Point presentation that he placed on a small cardboard pedestal. He nodded toward Feinberg, who then proceeded to go through the presentation, point by point, detailing the rising costs of healthcare in the United States and all the familiar numbers about the un-insured and under-insured. I felt like I was attending a congressional hearing before a Democrat-controlled committee. Then he began to explain their proposal.

"It's not a public option," said Feinberg, "but you might call it an alien option." He laughed, and his round belly shook while his double and triple chins expanded and contracted like an accordion.

"This next slide," Feinberg said, "gets to the heart of the matter. It's what we call the Shakespearean solution."

"Come again."

"First, we kill all the lawyers."

"Very funny," I replied.

"We're not joking," Al interjected.

"You simply can't have a functioning healthcare system with lawyers. So we would kill all of them," said Feinberg.

I think they could see my Adam's apple moving up and down and could tell that I was in a bit of shock.

"Oh, not to worry," Al said. "By lawyers, we refer only to litigators. The others would be grandfathered."

"Hey," said Feinberg, "that reminds me, have you heard the one about the lawyer, the rabbi and the taxidermist? You see, this lawyer kills a shark, and he takes it to—"

"Not now, Ben," said Al.

"Oh, okay, sorry. Anyway, yeah, the lawyers have got to go."

I had to admit that the idea of exterminating trial lawyers was not totally distasteful to me. I couldn't help thinking about Louis Sullivan, a notorious plaintiff's lawyer (obnoxious and arrogant in the extreme) who had made life miserable for several of my former clients in the automotive industry. I thought, fatuously, of asking if I could be present at some of the executions. Then I remembered that, early in my career, I had actually participated in several trials. I had been little more than a legal flunky—one of a team of young associates who had done tedious research and reviewed depositions. I'd been allowed to sit at counsel's table in the courtroom a few times, but certainly not permitted to speak. I wondered if they were unaware of these indiscretions or if they were only concerned with attorneys who currently were litigators. Or might there be a kind of inquisitor's panel that would examine every lawyer's history, so that I might be sealing my own fate if I agreed to this? I decided that I had better play my cards close to the vest for now. Plus, I could see that an emotional response—statements of shock, indignation and the like—would carry no weight with these guys.

"The numbers I have seen suggest that legal costs only represent 1 - 2% of medical inflation," I said.

Both men looked at each other and laughed. "Where did you get those statistics—from the American Bar Association?" Feinberg said.

"Well, I have to admit, I find them a bit hard to believe myself."

"Why do you think the doctors run all those tests on those expensive machines?" Feinberg asked.

"Well," I replied, "probably because they increasingly own the machines and get most of the money from the tests."

"That gets into the other part of the solution," Al said.

"And that would be?"

Al continued, "The doctors would all make a standard salary of $200,000. That's a lot less than the surgeons and some of the specialists make, but it's more than a lot of them are netting now after malpractice insurance and the expenses of processing government forms."

I thought of some of my friends who were orthopedic and heart surgeons and how they would react to a $200,000 salary—they'd probably lobby congress to fight to the last man standing before submitting to such a preposterous proposal. But what was really bothering me were the plans for lawyers. I got up from the table and walked behind my desk, where I pulled a plaque off the wall. I brought it back and placed it on the center of the table. "Do you see the name of the organization on this certificate?"

"We know that the American Bar Association isn't going to like every aspect of this," Al said.

"Yeah, especially the killing part," Feinberg inserted with a smirk.

"Couldn't we come up with something a bit less drastic?" I asked. "I mean, like quarantining them or something?"

"You can't do that," Al said. "Lawyers are like toadstools that sprout after spring showers. They'll just keep popping up unless we eliminate them. We're actually a bit reluctant to limit the . . . uh . . . sanctions to trial lawyers, but we figure we couldn't do a merger deal if we eliminate all attorneys."

"Are these deal points?" I asked.

"I'm afraid so," Al said. "And, unfortunately, we have to keep the 'EO' on the table."

"The 'EO'?" I asked.

"The Extinction Option," said Feinberg.

"If we can't come to a meeting of the minds, our other option," said Al, "is to make an example out of Earth. Simply extinguish it and use it as an example for the next planet that refuses to negotiate. But we really don't want to do that. We want you to help us build a template for interplanetary mergers of the future, and we want to make this a sort of laboratory where we can perfect the approach and then communicate best practices to other negotiators working in other galaxies. We're giving you the opportunity to be in on the ground-floor of this new model."

I nodded. I mean what could I do or say? I wasn't exactly dealing from a position of strength here.

"Back to the healthcare matter," Al said. "As I mentioned earlier, we tried to come up with what we could offer you as a sign of good faith—something that would be viewed most positively by folks on your planet, especially in this country. Fixing your healthcare system and killing the lawyers seemed to make a lot of sense."

He waited for a response, but I was too overwhelmed to say a word, so he continued. "I may not have made it clear, but healthcare will be free. We believe that, with the lawyers out of the way and a cap on doctors' salaries, and if we can avoid the expenses of a military campaign, we should be able to provide healthcare free of charge, especially since we'll be reducing our own healthcare costs by avoiding casualties. And of course, we'll be utilizing some of your planet's resources."

"Yeah, and the heads of state will all be offered consulting agreements and nice retirement packages," added Feinberg. "We don't have to worry about the compensation restrictions of your TARP program," he said with a self-satisfied smile. "They'll also have seats on an advisory board of directors."

It occurred to me that, with the exception of my spaceship sighting, I really had no proof that these characters could do what they said they could. "No offense, gentlemen, but what can you do in the way of establishing credibility?"

"You mean," asked Al, "how can we prove we can do what we say we can?"

"Something like that."

"Would you like an Hiroshima-type demonstration?"

I could sense that I needed to be very careful with my response. If I said "yes" would I be sealing the fates of millions of people who would die to help these guys make their point? I thought about things that my UFO club would like to see exterminated in a show of force: the UN Building, no doubt, would be high on the list, followed closely by ACLU headquarters. Our banker member would probably like to see the U.S. Treasury offices—especially the floors housing the TARP administrators—gone, while our doctor would love to see the Medicare offices nuked. I also remembered from my college history courses how scholars had criticized Truman for dropping bombs on the populations of Hiroshima and Nagasaki without a prior, non-lethal demonstration of the new weapons. Who would have thought that these studies would ever become truly relevant in my own life?

"I'd like to give some thought to what kind of demonstration would be meaningful," I responded, trying to buy time.

"Of course," Al replied. "We don't need to settle everything today."

"There is, however, one other item that I would like to discuss." The two men nodded in their best spirit of cooperation. "I hate to seem skeptical. I mean, I realize that I witnessed a very spectacular event last year—one that you went to great expense to prepare—but I find myself alternating between thinking about legal points and wondering if I am just hallucinating; that this is just all some kind of bizarre dream or prank or something."

"You want us to demonstrate our bona fides? To show our credentials, so to speak?"

"Yeah, something like that."

"I suppose," Al said, casting a professorial-like glance down his long nose at Feinberg, "that we could do something a bit supernatural."

"You have supernatural powers?" I asked, in a halting voice.

"Nothing so much as you might think," Al said, "but we do possess a few abilities that you don't."

I watched, transfixed, as he raised his hand and pointed a finger at my coffee cup, and then sat frozen as I observed the liquid bubbling. Al then turned to Feinberg, who next pointed his finger at the cup, causing the frothing liquid to instantly freeze.

"Okay," I said sheepishly. "That should about do it." Wendell, who had followed me to the conference table and was still sitting on my lap, had turned his head and was trying to burrow into my chest for protection. I wasn't sure which of the two of us was the more frightened, but his animal instincts only reinforced to me that there was plenty of reason to tread lightly.

"Forgive me if this sounds patronizing or silly," I continued, "but shall I assume that your race has special intelligence?"

"Not so much," said Al. "We're just a lot older civilization than yours. We actually have representatives in some of your institutions of higher learning, and we've picked up some useful things there."

"Yeah," Feinberg chimed in, "we've got a few students at Berkeley and Cal Tech. We figured we didn't need to worry about looking weird out there—nobody would notice." He laughed with a big belly laugh as his ample stomach rolled up and down.

"We calculate," Al said, "that in five to seven hundred years, your weaponry systems will approach the potency and versatility of ours, which is another reason why we can't dither on this deal forever."

I nodded, not wanting to appear thick-headed about what seemed to be such an obvious reality. "So, assuming that I agree to represent you, where do we go from here, gentlemen?" I wondered if "gentlemen" was the right word, but was clueless as to an appropriate substitute.

"Well," Al responded, "McKenzie is going to arrange some meetings for us in Washington, but we'd also like to meet with your UFO club to get some feedback from them."

"Feedback?" I asked.

"Yes, that's right. Although we've no reason to believe that we have not established credibility with McKenzie and Bain, we can't be absolutely certain, especially since we're paying them quite handsomely, and they're likely to agree with anything we say so long as that continues. Your UFO club members—especially those who, like you, saw the flying saucer last year—are more likely to take us seriously, and we do want to get a bit more input on some of our ideas. Call it a sort of customer focus group, if you like."

Al and Feinberg rose from the table in unison, the meeting apparently over.

"And how can I reach you?" I asked.

Al reached into the inside pocket of his suit coat, from which he extracted a business card. It read: "Alfred Collins, Chairman, Earth Studies Department, Institute de Planets."

The men made for the door, and Wendell and I accompanied them outside. I could see them gazing at the mountain ranges that circled Billings in what I had previously thought of as a sort of protective shield—the Bighorns, the Crazy Mountains and the Snowy Mountain ranges.

"So, where do you guys go next?" I asked.

"We're actually thinking of doing a bit of sightseeing," Feinberg replied.

"Yes," Al said, "we'd like to visit the site of the Battle of the Little Bighorn. I always like to talk about that in my classes, and I've not had the opportunity to actually visit the location."

The battle site was only sixty-five miles southeast—I had visited it many times—and I could suddenly envision in a much more concrete way how General Custer must have felt when he first realized how overwhelming were the forces of Sitting Bull that confronted his Seventh Cavalry. As the men approached their rental car, they turned around and looked back at me somewhat quizzically, seeming to focus their attention on Wendell, who was now pawing at my leg, wanting to be picked up. Surely they wouldn't think of harming him, I thought, but out of an abundance of caution, I pulled him up close to my chest, and he gave me a lick. We would go down together or not at all.

"I'll talk to the president of our UFO club about bringing some special visitors," I said.

"Until then," Al replied.

"Yes, until then."

CONTRIBUTORS

The Southern Indiana Writers Group has been more-or-less together since 1992. We began meeting monthly in a conference room in a local hospital. We now meet weekly to exchange information and expertise on everything from computers to poetry. The group also serves as a critique forum (in the same sense that a pack of wolves serves as food critics). Membership is limited, but visitors are welcome, and have been known to fit in so well they become members against their better judgment.

Bonnie Abraham After twenty-five plus years of writing letters disqualifying people from Unemployment Benefits, she retired in order to write something more pleasant. She writes short stories (many with Biblical themes), poetry and devotionals. Currently, she resides in Corydon with her mother's ghost.

Marian Allen lives in a big house in a little wood, which is not the only difference between Allen and Laura Ingels Wilder. She has published stories in print and on-line magazines, including Marion Zimmer Bradley's FANTASY Magazine, The Phone Book, PanGaia and Oceans of the Mind. She blogs at marianallen.com.

Jeannine Baumgartle writes poetry and fiction. Her work has appeared in publications such as *Green Meadow Press*, *Flying Island, Literally*, and Studio: *A Journal for Christians Writing* and won a residency for poetry at the Mary Anderson Center for the Arts . She and her husband live in the small town of Crandall.

Ginny Fleming considers herself to be foremost a screenwriter, as this is her favorite media. Because nobody thought to tell her she couldn't, after optioning 3 scripts for the unsold ensemble sitcom *"Tia"* (any producers reading this?), Fleming dived head-first into the shark-infested mulligan stew (How's that for mixing metaphors?) that is Hollywood scriptwriting. Fleming's take on hysterical fantasy (funny, that is), a novel she likes to call *Dragonsayver* (when she's not calling it Marvin), is a "Shrek-like" novel just begging to be made into an animated film (Fleming wonders if she should shove a tin cup in its hand and drop it on a busy intersection). Besides her annual contribution to SIW anthology and a brief appearance in the Louisville Courier-Journal, Fleming is busy finding a home for *Keys of Illusion*, a Romantic/Suspense novel filled with magic, scuba, fantasy, a bunch of lavender stuff and little bit of sex. Multiple scripts are always in the works whenever Fleming manages to "channel" Jimmy Buffett, her "Muse" (Yeah, she knows Jimmy's not dead — Hopes for his continued good health, in fact — That just makes him easier to channel).

Dirk Griffin, also known as The Invisible Man. Dirk is seldom among us in reality, but reality has never been our strong suit, anyway. He has written theatre reviews for Arts Kentuckiana, had a script produced for Public Access Television, and has written music/lyrics and/or scripts for several musicals. Bunbury Theatre of Louisville, Kentucky, selected one of Griffin's plays, *Plastic Jesus*, to include in their 2001 15th Anniversary 15 Minute Play Festival.

T Lee Harris is a writer and illustrator who has been a lover of mystery and the detective genre since discovering books. A graduate of Indiana University with a Bachelor of Fine Arts, T has been involved with radio production, game design, comic books and desktop publishing. Interests include participation in the Society for Creative Anachronism and Renaissance Faires, tailoring authentic costuming for re-enactors and playing online roleplaying games. Several novels are in progress featuring Sitehuti and Nefer-Djenou-Bastet, Josh Katzen and a series set in ninth century Ireland. Work has appeared in print and online venues including mystericale.com and Wildside Press' Cat Tales 2 anthology.

Joy Kirchgessner lives in Corydon with her husband, Mike. Her interests are too vast to list on this page. She's a long time business woman of Corydon, and artist, whose nature paintings have been accepted into prestigious shows, photographer, whose photographs have joined her illustrations in our anthologies, equestrian, who enjoys trail rides, amateur archaeologist, who enjoys rock hunting and exploring new worlds—give her a chemistry set and a laboratory and she'd try to split atoms. Many years ago, Southern Indiana Writers tied her to a computer and wonderful stories blossomed from Kirchgessner's many interests. So now, she must add accomplished writer to that long, long list. She even has a novel or two in the early stages.

Samantha Lopez grew up in Houston, Texas. She graduated from Southern Illinois University at Carbondale in Illinois, moved to Chicago, and is now in the Louisville area. When not fighting her two cats for the computer, she browses bookstores, practices various musical instruments, volunteers at sci-fi conventions, and attends Renaissance festivals. She writes science fiction, fantasy, mainstream, and poetry. Her poetry has been published in Nightlife newspaper. She is currently working on several novels.

Glenda Mills resides in New Albany, Indiana with her husband and youngest son. She has a daughter and a son who no longer live at home and one grandchild. When she is not busy homemaking, homeschooling, attending soccer games, running the family taxi service, or volunteering at her church, she writes fiction, nonfiction, and poetry. She looks forward to the day when a person can actually be in two places at once.

Ardis Moonlight quite naturally is a fan of the moon and stars, and finally can see it all in Harrison County, a plus after 32 years in Louisville! A poet with poems published in several issues of "Calliope", an anthology published yearly by Women Who Write, she is also trying her imagination with short stories, and….gasp…considering a novel!

Carl Page, an attorney and bank human resources director, is currently seeking a publisher for his recently completed novel: a thriller about a bank CEO who is blackmailed into assisting a Hezbollah cell with money laundering.

OTHER TITLES IN THE
INDIAN CREEK ANTHOLOGY SERIES:

Indian Creek Anthology
Ghost Writers
Christmas Bizarre
Dragon: Our Tales
Grounds for Suspicion
2000 Tales
Way Out West
Unbridled Lust
There's Something Under the Bedtime Stories
Novel Ingredients
Write of Passage
Off the Rack
Beastly Tales
It's Always Something
Most Wanted

Also by Southern Indiana Writers' Group:

Ghosts: On the Square . . . And Elsewhere . . . .

Visit our web site for excerpts of previous publications
and availability information:

http://southernindianawriters.com